THE GREAT DINOSAUR ROBBERY

If Quincey de Bapeau Charmaine-Bott, 25th Earl of Hastings and Queen's courier, hadn't collapsed at the foot of the American Museum of Natural History, and died at the feet of his old nanny, Hettie MacPhish, the population of Red China would even now be preparing for their Great Leap Downward.

But he had, leaving only a last-gasp clue to the hiding place of a secret message – a microdot containing the plans for a terrible threat to Western civilization. And that was why, on a hot summer's day in New York, a band of British nannies chose to steal one of the largest creatures ever to roam this earth – a sixty-six-feet long BRONTOSAURUS.

Also by the same author

And to my nephew Albert I leave the island what
I won off Fatty Hagan in a poker game

and available in Coronet Books

The Great Dinosaur Robbery

David Forrest

CORONET BOOKS
Hodder Paperbacks Ltd., London

Copyright © 1970 by David Eliades
and Robert Forrest Webb
First printed 1970 for Hodder & Stoughton Ltd
Coronet edition 1971

The authors wish to thank the American Museum
of Natural History and New York's 20th Police
Precinct for their help and amusing advice while
researching this book.

Printed and bound in Great Britain for
Coronet Books, Hodder Paperbacks Ltd,
St. Paul's House, Warwick Lane,
London, E.C.4
by Hunt Barnard Printing Ltd.,
Aylesbury, Bucks.

ISBN 0 340 15680 5

Memorandum

FROM: The pen of your enlightened Chairman,
Mao Tse-tung.
TO: The Department of Geophysical
Research, Peking Academy of Sciences.

Comrades:

Following the success of Republican China's
Great Leap Forward, I now present my
programme for the conquest of the Capitalist
West and their running dogs; diligently
applied, it will enable us to triumph,
WITHOUT resorting to open warfare - with its
inherent risks to ourselves of nuclear
retaliation. Code name for this operation
is The Great Leap Downward, and it is based
on the following principle: If, as the
earth's natural vibrations pass through our
beloved country, our entire population of
750,000,000 were to jump to the ground from
a height of about six feet, the resulting
increase of tremors would be carried across
the Pacific. Huge ground quakes and tidal
waves would sweep over the whole of the
United States' West Coast, destroying
everything. Island countries such as
Britain, and the whole of Northern Europe,
would be devastated. Neither would the
Soviet revisionists be spared. The forces of
nature would be blamed. And the world would
be ours.

(cont/d.)

However, in order that we may achieve best results, it is imperative that The Great Leap Downward is made at the time when the earth's vibrations are at their peak. I am assured they will reach their highest level of the century sometime this year. The duty of your Department is to notify me of the month, the day, the hour, and the very second when this maximum tremor is expected. Then, with the aid of our local party leaders and controllers, we will instruct my obedient followers, who will climb to the top of their jumping platforms and await my signal to leap.

CAUTION: If the Western countries learn of our scheme to use a geophysical weapon, they may be inspired to reverse the result by getting their own population to jump at the critical moment. Therefore, the keyword for our success is SECRECY.

Your beloved Chairman,
Mao Tse-tung

Hors d'œuvre

There's an English Earl among the exhibits of the American Museum of Natural History in New York. He is Quincey de Bapeau Charmaine-Bott, the 25th Earl of Hastings—the prized result of nine hundred years of selective breeding within Britain's dwindling herd of aristocracy.

But, as a majestic rose is grafted on to the rootstock of the common briar in order to attain its full beauty, so the Earl's ancestry goes back to a peasant farmer with the largest dungheap in the whole of Normandy. In fact, in the year A.D. 1065, the fumes rising from the rancid sewage just outside Rene Bott's hovel were so thick that even flies were reluctant to settle.

Six weeks of continuous rain in the early spring had softened the stinking mound, so that it spread across the yard till it lay slopping, several inches deep, in front of Rene Bott's doorway. It continually amazed him that only six sows and a boar had produced such an astonishing amount. He felt it was a pity that there was less of a market for pig-dung than for bacon.

Rene Bott, and his home, stank. He didn't wear shoes, so his gnarled toes gathered the soggy manure and deposited much of it in his living quarters, where it carpeted the stamped earth.

The water he drew from the well, only ten metres from the pig midden, was suspiciously brown. He used it for drinking. It was too dirty to wash in—so he didn't wash.

When William of Normandy decided to invade England and began gathering his army, villages throughout the countryside each nominated a man to serve. Unanimously, the village of Petit Bapeau nominated Bott. They'd wondered for years how they could rid themselves of the odious fog that hung over their valley. To them, the war was a godsend.

Bott was marched, at the end of a ten-foot-long catchpole, to the duckpond. He was soaked for three hours, then scrubbed with birch besoms and lye, until his flesh shone a bright, polished pink. But the pig smell lingered on. Despite this, the people of Petit Bapeau considered him fit to serve their King.

After ten weeks of intensive training, in preparation for the invasion of England, Sergeant Paul L'Apout described Rene Bott as follows: Lazy, untidy, dirty, smelly, inefficient, mean, totally useless as a pikeman, lacking any form of courage or skill, and fit only as a second-rate guard for the army's livestock, providing that it was livestock that he, Sergeant Paul L'Apout, wasn't expected to eat.

Rene Bott became a muleteer. His job was to lead the animals, laden with spare bows and arrows, up from the beach-head at Pevensey Bay. Naturally, he was closely—but not too closely—supervised by Sergeant L'Apout.

It was the fourteenth day of October, 1066, a warm afternoon. The forward soldiery had been fighting since dawn, and the defending army was split into small groups, battling around temporary palisades. Bott's skin was leaking sweat as he unloaded bundles of arrows from his mule team. He stacked them alongside the spare bows piled against an oak tree in a copse. He was taking a brief rest, before unpacking the last of his mules, when a squealing grunt startled him. A wild boar, panicked by the noise of the nearby battle, charged into the thicket. It stopped eight feet away from Bott. For a few seconds it hesitated, recognising the smell of a herd of pigs, but mystified by the sight of a man. Bott's tongue flicked around his lips. Greedily, he calculated the profit he would make from his hungry comrades, and grabbed the nearest bow. He slotted an arrow to the bowstring, and hauled back his powerful arm. He took a step to the left, to get in a broadside shot. It was characteristic of Rene Bott that he should trip over his ill-fastened cross-gartering at that critical moment. His mis-directed arrow ricocheted with a clang off the French Sergeant L'Apout's iron nosepiece, giving him thereafter permanently-raised eyebrows, whistled upwards through a flight of pigeons, and began its descent.

History records that the English knight, Sir Henry Beagle-ditch, ever concerned for his liege's spotless public image, remarked, at that instant of battle:

"Your Majesty, beware . . . A flock of pigeons flyeth overhead."

King Harold looked up. Rene Bott's arrow struck. Harold fell dead.

Two men changed their names that day. William of Normandy became William the Conqueror of England. Rene Bott was dug, barely alive, from the bog where he'd been thrown by the arrow-dented Sergeant L'Apout, and was elevated to the peerage by the grateful King William. He became the first Earl of Hastings. He altered his name to Rene de Bapeau Charmaine (after his favourite sow) -Bott, and was given a large parcel of English ground. He also secured a generous pension, and a position at the King's right elbow—the latter on condition that he bathed publicly at Yuletide and on Midsummer's Day.

The de Bapeau Charmaine-Botts became staunchly British, defenders of the Crown in war and peace. Every generation served the realm, and many heads of the family lost their lives in royal service. Several de Bapeau Charmaine-Botts died in the Crusades, others at Agincourt, Bannockburn, Crecy, Bosworth and in a dozen other battles.

When war became a middle-class occupation, the family turned to diplomacy. Sons were educated at Eton and Oxford, and fought for the British cause in embassies abroad.

Daughters ALWAYS married financiers.

The last of the male line of de Bapeau Charmaine-Botts is the Earl in the New York Natural History Museum. But unlike many of the exhibits, he is standing outside a glass case—looking in. He is twenty-eight years old, and is frequently named in *The Tailor and Cutter* as England's best-dressed nobleman. In the *London Illustrated News* and the social columns, he is described as the country's most eligible bachelor. And, in British Foreign Office memos, as the most reliable, trustworthy, discreet and fearless wearer of the Silver Greyhound, the insignia of the Queen's Couriers.

1

The 25th Earl is leaning on his umbrella—tightly rolled, cavalry style—in the main hall of the museum. His narrow face is sun-tanned beneath his curly-brimmed bowler. He has just arrived from Hawaii.

He looks at the museum clock, then checks it against the gold pocket-watch chained to his waistcoat. He has six minutes and thirty-one seconds before he meets his contact.

He swings the umbrella behind his back, paces over to the Theodore Roosevelt showcases, and stands there for a moment. He appears to be examining the president-explorer's buckskin clothing, but in reality he's keeping a lookout behind him in the plate glass of the display. Not that he's nervous—the de Bapeau Charmaine-Botts are noted for the iciness of their sang-froid while facing danger, and the 25th Earl, Queen's Courier, has faced it many times. He's watchful because he carries microfilm of Chairman Mao's plans for the Great Leap Downward, and he's been told that Mao ordered the Tse Eih Aei, the sinister Chinese spy network, to use any means to stop the secret from being blown. He is cautious also because he knows the way these Chinese agents work. The six Britons who successfully ferried the information out of Peking all subsequently died hideous, vengeful deaths. That's why the 25th Earl now carries a cyanide phial wedged in his cheek. What he doesn't know, however, is that the man he is waiting for in the museum is *also* dead—murdered and buried ten minutes ago in four small boxes in the Canine Garden of Rest, and bewailed by four theatrically tearful groups of Oriental mourners.

* * * .

The 25th Earl casually flipped the middle button of his Savile Row Suit and looked at his pocket-watch again. Five more minutes. He tapped his heels together and strolled, past the information desk, towards the other entrance on West 77th Street.

The giant-sized Haida-Indian canoe creaked as he passed. The Earl's eyes hardened. He gripped his umbrella a little tighter. A shadow moved. The Earl ducked, and a bone-tipped war lance hissed through the air and stuck, quivering, in the body of a stuffed bear. He hung his umbrella on the shaft and turned to face the boat. The dugout crew of painted braves came to life, climbed over the side of the boat, and slowly, in a grim and silent half-circle, moved towards him.

There was the chatter of a party of rescuing school-children. The Earl's attackers hesitated as the footsteps approached. Then they scrambled back into the boat to resume their previous poses as slave paddlers. The children, schoolteachers and guides appeared. The 25th Earl retrieved his umbrella, nodded to a schoolmistress, who eyed the im-paled bear suspiciously. He sprinted up the stairs, keeping close to the wall. He made for the auditorium. From the darkness came a hiccupping sound, and a bullet picked at his sleeve. "Dammit," he thought, "They're closing in." He ducked into a side hall, glanced around quickly, and pulled a neat Georgian silver snuff-box from his waistcoat pocket. He flicked it open and shook a miniscule red and white striped cylinder into his hand. He studied the monster ex-hibit and vaulted on to the plinth. He reached up and dropped the cylinder into the mouth of the largest of the beasts.

He stepped off, smoothed down his jacket, adjusted his

shirtcuff length and checked his tie knot. He smiled. Now it was safe. He'd collect later, and rearrange the hand-over.

Quincey de Bapeau Charmaine-Bott smiled again. Not long, now, and he'd be back in Hawaii, with the sun and the sophisticated young American heiress he'd left by the swimming pool of the Surfrider. Skirting the long hall which had hidden the gunman, and avoiding exhibits which could conceal further attackers, the 25th Earl reached the exit facing Central Park West.

A drably-clothed Oriental tourist moved towards him. Sunlight slanted off the tall walls of the building by the Theodore Roosevelt equestrian statue. The 25th Earl paused to accustom his eyes to the brilliant glare. Then he straightened his regimental tie and began a brisk walk down the steps. Half way, he looked back towards the entrance.

He trod on something soft, stumbled slightly and grabbed a well-rounded body for support.

"M-M-Madam ... most f-f-frightfully ..." he began. A stout children's nurse, grey-haired and considerably affronted by having her bosom strangled, let go the handle of her push-chair and hit him across the side of his face with her handbag.

"How dare you, you sex maniac!" roared her Scots-accented voice.

"G-G-Good God, N-N-Nanny Hettie," gasped the 25th Earl.

The nanny looked. Her eyes squinted. "My, my ... Maister Quincey!" she said. Her voice hardened, slightly. "And who taught you to be a rapist blackguard?" She stooped and rubbed her ankle. "Kicking your nanny ..." She stood, tried her weight on the foot, then smiled at him. "Wheesht, and look at you—a Laird, perspiring in public!"

"N-N-Nanny ... S-S-Sorry ... A-A-Accident ... N-N-Nanny Hettie ... b-but y-y-you ... you ..."

"Don't stutter, laddie."

"You really shouldn't h-ha-have h-h-hit me, Nanny," said the 25th Earl, his face pale. "You've just c-c-c-crushed my suicide pill." He delicately felt his cheek, with his fingertips.

"Och! Nonsense," exclaimed the nurse. "Away with your silly games, Maister Quincey."

"I've got l-l-less than s-s-s-sixty seconds to live. P-P-Poison. Thank heaven I can rely on you to deliver a m-m-message. No, don't interrupt me." He turned to the young nurse accompanying the Scotswoman.

"You have a timepiece? Yes? Well, start a c-c-countdown, p-p-please. Start now ... at f-f-fifty ... forty-five." He looked at his own watch, again. The young woman began.

"Forty-five ... forty-four ... forty-three ..."

The Scots nanny's face coloured. She looked at him, threateningly. "Maister Quincey. Now see here, laddie ..."

The 25th Earl took her arm, gently. "D-D-Don't interrupt m-me, p-p-p-please, Nanny Hettie," he begged. "Just listen. It's vital. V-VERY important ... it's g-g-government work ... d-d-d-don't have much time ..."

"Fifteen ... fourteen ... thirteen ..." counted the young nanny.

"W-W-World security ... avoid t-t-total destruction ... m-m-museum ... the m-m-message ... microdot ... room th-thirteen ... largest beast ... don't t-t-trust anyone ..." The 25th Earl's jaw stiffened. He struggled to speak. "Get it to ... to ..."

"Three. Two. One," said the nurse-timekeeper. "Zero."

The young Earl drew himself to attention. His eyes focused on the distance. He saluted. "G-G-God save the Q-Q-Queen," he gasped, collapsing rigidly backwards.

"Good grief," said Nanny Hettie. She looked down at him. "Maister Quincey. Maister Quincey. Stop playing games. THIS MINUTE," she commanded. Had he been alive, the 25th Earl wouldn't have dared to disobey.

"Maister Quincey ..." The Scotswoman bent anxiously over the prostrate figure and lifted its wrist. She felt for the pulse. A small knot of visitors gathered around them.

"Is he?" asked the young nanny, her eyes wide.

Her companion clamped an ear to the Earl's chest. Then

she squatted back on her heels.

"Oh, God, we're afraid he is," she said, quietly. "Oh, dearie us. Poor Maister Quincey, what have we done? He was such a bonnie bairn."

An Oriental-looking spectator leant forward. He looked at the nannies. "Physician," he said, running his hands swiftly over the corpse.

"Okay ... okay ... okay ... Break it up, now. Get moving ..." A New York policeman shouldered his way through the growing crowd. "Okay, let me get to him. You, nurse," he said, looking at the stout Scotswoman. "You go call a meat wagon."

*   *   *

Nanny Hettie MacPhish, sixty-year-old ex-royal nanny, had assumed, throughout her working life, so many of her employers' names that she frequently forgot her own. Currently, she was Nanny Badenberg, working for Walter Badenberg, the New York industrialist. Over the years she'd been Nanny Trent, nurse for the Nottinghamshire barons; Nanny Norfolk, when she nurtured the Duke's offspring; Nanny Derby; then Nanny Hastings, with Master Quincey. But most glorious of all, she'd been Nanny Windsor—royal Nanny Windsor. Her close friends noticed that, ever since the glorious day of her appointment to the crowned family, she'd also adopted the royal plural in her speech. Now, she NEVER referred to herself as 'I'—it was always 'We'.

"Watch the bairn a moment," she told Melissa, her young companion. She kicked on the brake of young Simone's push-chair and hurried to the telephone kiosk. After she'd phoned, she stood and listened to the siren as the long Plymouth wove through the traffic towards the museum. She watched the white-coated men jog up the steps and push their way through the persistent crowd around the 25th Earl. Seconds later, they carried his body into the ambulance. The policeman stood on the steps, jotting notes in his pocketbook. The crowd thinned and disappeared. After a minute, there was no sign of anything unusual having happened. She walked back towards Melissa. The policeman stopped her.

"I'd like your name, ma'am."

She nodded, and told him.

"We might like a statement later," said the policeman, writing down her address in his book. "Must have been a heart attack. Heat, perhaps. Thank you for your help, ma'am." He saluted her, vaguely.

Hettie swallowed. Master Quincey had been one of her favourite children. She remembered his clumsy, comic first steps. She thought for a moment. She could remember even earlier, when he'd been carried out of the delivery room, and handed into her arms. Now, he was dead. It wasn't possible. She hadn't even seen him for years, although he'd never forgotten to send her gifts at Christmas and on her birthdays.

Nannies aren't emotional, she reminded herself. She took a deep breath and clenched her fists. "Steady, Hettie, old lass," she said, quietly. "Chin up, chest out, firm step. There's work to be done." She was sure that a Charmaine-Bott would only be involved in something very necessary.

She looked up the steps to the museum. An important message, Master Quincey had said with his dying words. Hettie gulped. Of WORLD importance. It HAD to be delivered. It was in room thirteen.

The young nanny was sitting on the museum steps, very pale. Hettie thought of correcting her for getting dirt on her uniform, but she stopped herself. She rested a hand on the girl's shoulder. "It's all right, Melissa," she said softly. "Just sit quietly for a few minutes. Wait for us, we're going inside the museum." Melissa nodded.

Hettie adjusted the strap round baby Simone's waist, and straightened the child's sun bonnet, then she climbed the steps to the museum entrance. Room thirteen, Master Quincey had said. She looked for an attendant.

"Sure, lady, you mean the Early Dinosaur Hall," said the uniformed man. "Everyone wants the Dinosaur Hall. You know, lady, that dinosaur's nearly two hundred millions of years old. You get that? Millions. Take the elevator. Fourth floor."

The Scots nanny took the lift to the fourth floor. Room thirteen, its number in gold paint, was easy to find. Hettie remembered more of the 25th Earl's last words. ". . . Message . . . microdot . . . In largest beast . . ." She looked inside the room. "Lawks!" she exclaimed. "The dear laddie could hardly have chosen anything bigger." She walked in. Dominating the centre of the hall, and flanked by two lesser giants, was the fossilised skeleton of one of the largest creatures ever to roam this earth—a brontosaurus.

Hettie made her way to the limestone plinth on which the three petrified monsters stood. She glanced about her. There were two visitors at the far end of the hall. She waited until they had gone, then she squeezed under the guard-rail and climbed on to the plinth, close to the head of the sixty-six-feet-long brontosaurus. She listened for a moment, to make sure no one was near. Then, gritting her teeth and holding back a shudder, she stuck her hand into the beast's jaws and felt around. She found nothing. She was surprised. It seemed the obvious place to hide a message. She looked for another hiding place. Inside the rib cage, perhaps? She searched as carefully as she could, again with no success. Puzzled, she examined the tail bones. She tried to visualise the size of the message. She recalled the 25th Earl's words. "A microdot," he'd said. Would that be bigger than a pea? She decided it would probably be smaller. It must be pushed into one of the bones, then. There were hundreds. It could be anywhere. She made another fruitless search. Then came the sound of approaching footsteps.

Hettie sighed. Sadly, she left the hall.

*   *   *

William Badenberg boasts that he is 2,922 today. Days, that is. Actually, he's eight years old, and he's enjoying himself. Birthdays are one of the few times when he sees his mother and father together. They're not divorced. It's just that Mr. Badenberg is always busy being successful.

"It's William's birthday on Tuesday," Mrs. Badenberg cabled him in Zurich.

"Fine," Mr. Badenberg cabled back. "Fix him a cocktail party. Buy him a new car."

"At eight?" cabled Mrs. Badenberg.

"At any suitable time," replied her husband.

A telephone call to his Swiss office ended the confusion. Mr. Badenberg cancelled forty-three appointments, took two days from work, and flew home.

William has twenty guests, suitably chosen from Mrs. Badenberg's social blue book, and all children of the right sort of people to know.

They are enjoying a lobster barbecue on the Badenberg patio. They are being entertained. They like Sammy Davis Jnr., Danny Kaye and Julie Andrews. Mr. Badenberg is glad he hired them. He knows that, otherwise, he wouldn't have known how to entertain one child—let alone this lot. He is standing beside the french windows, anaesthetising his conscience with Martinis. He is feeling guilty about his neglected business.

Mrs. Badenberg flicks her teeth with an elegant fingernail. She's worried. She's wondering if the nannies' champagne has been correctly chilled.

The nannies are a social conundrum. Mrs. Badenberg often discusses them with her friends. The nannies are efficient, polite, perfectly mannered and correct, but diffident. They never mix with their employers—even when encouraged. They prefer their own, élite, company.

*   *   *

While their charges giggled at Danny Kaye, the nannies

sat and chatted in the lounge. They sipped the champagne, and nibbled cracker biscuits generously coated with caviar. They seemed relaxed, but Mrs. Badenberg knew their lynx-eyes missed nothing. She hoped she'd chosen the right year.

Mrs. Badenberg popped her head round the door of the lounge and looked. As usual, they sat in small knots, chatting quietly. No matter how often the nannies met, the cliques remained unchanged. They weren't grouped by ages or salaries. She could understand a social gap caused by nationality, but these nannies were ALL British. She whispered to her own nurse.

"Everything satisfactory?"

"Perfectly, ma'am," nodded Nanny Hettie. Mrs. Badenberg left, pulled the door closed behind her, shrugged, and joined the children on the patio.

"Terrible, terrible thing to happen," said Hettie, resuming her interrupted narrative. The other nannies in her five-strong coterie nodded in sympathy. "Poor, dear wee Maister Quincey. And after all these years. Such wonderful people, too, the de Bapeau Charmaine-Botts."

"Very thad, Nanny Hettie," lisped Susanne Martyn, the youngest nurse of her group, her blonde hair streaky from the reflected white of her uniform.

"We brought him up. He had dreadful measles ... and mumps. But he was always very brave."

"He must have been. He passed on heroically," said Melissa, the nanny who had made the countdown on the museum steps. "You could tell he'd had the right sort of training. Quite calm and collected. Really a credit to you, Nanny Hettie."

The old nanny shook her head. "Not really, lassie. It's blood that matters. We do our best, but without the right blood ... nothing."

The other nannies nodded again.

"Foreign Office, wasn't he?" asked Emily Biddle, the oldest member of Hettie's clique. Her hair stood out like porcupine quills. She blinked through a pair of pince-nez. "I can remember his grandfather. Victoria Cross—Zulu War, I think."

Melissa leant forward, confidentially. "The Earl said he was doing something VERY important when he died. He said ..." A sharp jab from Hettie's elbow cut her in mid-sentence.

"But, he ..."

"Nothing," said Hettie, firmly. "What he said was quite private."

Melissa bit her lip. The other nannies nodded in agreement with Hettie. What the 25th Earl had said at his moment of death was no one else's business but his nanny's.

*　　　*　　　*

Nanny Hettie MacPhish had three layers of bags under her eyes. She hadn't been sleeping. Every time she'd closed her eyelids, she could see the 25th Earl's face. Every time she'd tried to rest, she could hear his voice giving her his last instructions.

She walked her baby carriage in the morning sunlight. Master William, suffering from party stomach, was at school. His sister, two-year-old Simone, waved a fresh teddy-bear at passers-by. Mrs. Badenberg insisted there was nothing more unhygienic than a dirty teddy-bear. "Simone must have a new one every day," she ordered. "Out of the plastic wrapper in the morning—into the trashcan at night."

Hettie didn't agree, of course. Who ever heard of anyone throwing away a teddy-bear? How could a child grow to love a teddy this way? Still, every employer had her foible. Hettie partly obeyed Mrs. Badenberg, and placed a regular order at Macy's store. But she didn't throw away the used bears. By Christmas, she calculated, she'd have nearly two hundred to send to the children's hospital.

Until the 25th Earl's death, the bears, sitting in waiting regiments along the shelves lining her small apartment, had eyed her with affection. Now, she felt, their once-friendly faces showed mistrust.

Forty-three years a nanny, thought Hettie. Forty-three years since she was seventeen. Six satisfied families, including a period with the royal family. Five perfect references. She reached forward and checked the push-chair safety straps, tidied the coverlet and bunched the pillow behind Simone. The face of the 25th Earl stared up at her.

She aimed her push-chair at the park gates and along the path towards the seat where she would meet her friends. They were already there. They sat, like four white slats of picket fencing, on the long seat facing the Delacorte Alice-in-Wonderland monument.

Old Emily was knitting another waistcoat for Tarzan, her pet parrot. He was as eccentric as his owner, and nervous. He'd been reared in front of a television set. He was unable to speak, or whistle, but gave a convincing imitation of his jungle namesake—and he'd plucked his chest naked. Emily spent all her spare moments knitting him gay, miniature waistcoats to replace his colourful feathers and keep out the chill, while Tarzan dedicated his life to unknitting each new psychedelic garment. It was an endless competition for both of them. Emily daily devised intricate new stitches which she hoped were unravellable. But by bedtime each evening, Tarzan was naked again. He'd sidle along the perch and swing upside-down on the bars until Emily dressed him in his new woolly. He'd sleep warm and cosy on his swing, then, with his ape-man yodel, would begin his sartorial beak-work the following dawn.

"Good morning." The nannies nodded a welcome, like a row of porcelain Buddhas.

Hettie smiled, thinly. The four friends shuffled along, so she could join them on the bench. She parked the carriage and set the brake.

"Didnae sleep," she said.

"It'll take time, dear," replied Emily.

The other three nannies nodded again.

"No," sighed Hettie. "It's no just Maister Quincey's

death. It's something else. We must tell you. We need your advice."

She explained exactly what had happened on the museum steps and the last words of the 25th Earl.

"There you are," exclaimed Melissa, dramatically. "He really *was* a British spy! Spies always carry suicide pills."

Hettie was shocked. "Spy? Away with you. Charmaine-Botts would never be spies. The Silver Greyhound. We saw it, behind his lapel. He was a royal courier. Spy, indeed! Really! He was delivering a message. It must have been for Her Majesty the Queen."

"Well, my dear," said Emily, kindly. "You really mustn't blame yourself for his death. I'm sure the queen would understand. But what are you going to do? Tell the British Ambassador?"

"No," said Hettie, firmly. "Maister Quincey said not to trust ANYONE. We're sure he wouldn't have meant you, of course," she added, hastily. "You're friends. Good friends." Hettie dabbed at her eyes with her handkerchief. "It was his dying wish, you know," she said. "That message must be very important. It's just got to be found and sent to the queen."

"By registered post," added Una. "That'll be safe."

Emily's pince-nez dropped from her nose, as she nodded, enthusiastically. She fumbled for them on her lap, amongst the confusion of her knitting wool, then tugged at the cord that suspended them from her neck, reeling them in like a fisherman. "Yes. AND I'll help you to find it."

The nannies' heads wagged agreement. "We'll ALL help," said Susanne.

*　　*　　*

On, across the wilds of Central Park, advanced the small British contingent. The nannies always marched, never strolled, backs straight, heads up, chins pulled well back on to their chests. And they marched in column, in order of seniority.

Hettie led them … because she had been a royal nanny. Her buxom figure and broad back almost obscured the view of her second-in-command, Emily. Behind the leaders strode Una, middle-aged and allergic to men, followed by the red-headed Melissa, and, as long as she could keep up with them, seventeen-year-old Susanne.

The eyes of the natives watched them.

"Der sterilised, Charlie," whispered one of the watchers, as the column strode past.

"Don' be 'diculous. Dames ain't sterilised. Only cats."

"Nuts! I mean like an operatin' theatre. Like when they castrated me."

"Circumstanced you, you mean."

"Yeah, that too." The heads turned and watched as the last of the nanny squadron disappeared round a bend in the path.

It was a bright morning, with just enough breeze coming in from the sea to clear the automobile fumes and smoke mist from around the tall buildings at the end of the park. The previous evening's rain had washed the dust from the leaves and grass, and the park had a fresh, rinsed look.

The nannies trundled their carriages along the side of the boating lake and through the tree-lined groves to Central Park West. By the time they'd arrived, they felt sticky and damp under their starched board-like aprons.

Hettie stopped opposite the American Museum and pushed the traffic light button on the crossing in front of the building. A small jam of carriage-pushing nannies built up behind her.

The crossing lights changed to green. A tattered yellow cab grated to a halt. The driver leant out of the window.

"You chicks a parade or sumpting?" he called. The nannies stuck their noses into the air and ignored him. Una blushed.

They parked their carriages by the steps at the front of the yellowstone building. "Knowledge" declared huge

23

letters over the museum entrance.

"Susanne, wait here." Hettie pointed towards the base of the Theodore Roosevelt statue guarding the entrance. "Watch all the perambulators. And take care of the children. Don't talk to any strange men, and if you want to sit down, then sit with your back straight."

Skirting the spot on the steps where the 25th Earl died, Hettie led the others into the shadows of the great entrance hall. It was quiet, almost churchlike, after the noise outside. The sun shone through the heavily-screened windows behind them. The stone columns threw long shadows ahead.

"Ugh!" gasped Una, looking at two primitive, carved wooden heads, on pillars, in front of them. She shuddered. There was something almost evil about these ebony guardians to the upper floors of the building.

Hettie ordered her squad up to the fourth floor.

"Just along here," she hissed.

The corridor grew darker. At last Hettie stopped outside a large doorway.

"Here. This is it. This is the place Maister Quincey hid the message in." Hettie nodded towards the panelled opening. "It's in there."

They crowded beside her and peered into the half gloom. "Oh, Lord," said Una. "What a terrible thing."

"It's horrible," breathed Melissa.

"And huge," said Emily, holding her pince-nez away from her nose like lorgnettes. "It's a dinosaur."

The prehistoric monster's craggy, sepia-coloured head, as big as a rubbish bin, snarled down at them. Its back arched upwards to a gigantic rump, twelve feet above the nineteen-ton slab of limestone plinth. Rib cages, like the unfinished hull of a Viking sailing ship, were supported by brown leg bones, each almost as big as the nannies themselves. The castellated tail drooped down and seemed to go on forever.

Hettie stepped back from the display and tried to view the entire monster from farther away. Then she beckoned her friends until they were huddled in a tight group. She glanced towards the monster. "He said it was in there. At least, he said it was in the largest exhibit. This is the biggest. If Maister Quincey said it was there, then it has to be. He never fibbed. It's in there, or ON there. Some sort of a message, somewhere."

The four nannies searched. For an hour and a half they examined the dinosaur. They poked, prodded and peered. They looked from a distance when other visitors or an attendant entered the hall. But when they were alone, they climbed on to the plinth and scuttled around the skeleton.

They found nothing. At last, they gave up the hunt.

2

The entrance to the New York headquarters of the Tse Eih Aei, Red China's espionage service, is by means of the middle telephone box in the block of three in front of the Plaza Hotel. Drop a coin into the instrument, dial 834927, press the concealed knob behind the cable outlet, and you are lowered into a damp and clammy room in an underground alley off one of the main sewers. The room stinks of joss sticks, opium and alligator chop-suey. It is made habitable only by the smell of perfumed bathwater and high-class sewage from the hotel.

The room is badly lighted, and steam from the sewer condenses on everything, dribbling in rivulets down the mildewed walls. Boots, shoes and leather belts turn mouldy green in a few days. Spy cameras grow exotic fungi on their lenses. But this HQ has advantages; it's reasonably central, near the subway and bus routes, and, most important of all, it costs nothing. Dollars are preciously guarded by the Chinese People's Republic.

The twelve-foot-square room is crammed and cramped. Six bunks, in tiers of three, line two opposing walls, like berths in an opium den. A third wall holds the radio transmitter and receiver, topped by a large, crayoned poster quoting Mao Tse-tung's 1964 exhortation to the Congolese: "People of the World, unite and defeat the U.S. aggressors and all their running dogs ... Monsters of all kinds shall be destroyed."

The fourth wall is shortened by the passage leading into the sewer, and by the entrance to the small lift. A coin-operated spin-drier and an electric cooker stand close by. Two curling pictures of Mao Tse-tung stand on shelves on this wall, above the drier and the stove, and between pots and pans used for preparing the spies' meals.

The centre of the room is occupied by a warped plywood table, its edges frayed with cigarette burns, its centre stained by tea-cup rings. There are only six chairs, filched from the open-air theatre in Central Park. There's no room for a seventh, so at full meetings, one of the agents has to sit in the background, on a bunk, or on the spin-drier.

There is a meeting on at present. The language is Cantonese. Wo Dung, who was in charge of the party assigned to capture the message from the 25th Earl, is making his report.

"Then, this long-nosed white devil ... how would you describe him, comrades? Perhaps as one of the mountain lake lotus-blossoms, enveloping in delicate leaves the deadly haspnich beetle? He sidesteps adroitly, and therefore my well-cast lance passes within the thousandth of a millimetre of his heart. And he runs like a forest hare up the balustraded staircase of the lower museum section."

"So ... ?" sighed Lui Ho, the group leader and political commissar.

"However, Comrade Leader," interrupted the sarcastic tones of Fat Choy. "Wo Dung did score a minor triumph.

His well-cast lance transfixed a bear—a RUSSIAN bear."

Lui Ho's skeletal face showed neither pleasure nor anger. He reached into his coat pocket and withdrew a copy of the Quotations from Chairman Mao Tse-tung. He placed it on the table in front of him, and studied the red plastic cover. Fat Choy noticed that the exact centre of Lui Ho's bald head was beginning to change colour. It was the spy-squad's only indication of their leader's humour. The centre of his pate chameleoned to a maroonish yellow. Lui Ho was angry.

Wo Dung, the second-in-command, failed to notice the ominous warning. He giggled as he continued. "And then, dear Comrade Leader, our Indian braves ... You should have seen them in their warpaint. They attacked, but were frustrated by a woman ... a schoolteacher. I would have killed her, but she had many children with her. Therefore, I ordered the warriors back to the ship."

"So ... ?" sighed Lui Ho, his scalp colour now nearing purple.

Wo Dung smiled. "But, oh, illustrious War Lord, our closely pursued enemy agent committed a fatal manoeuvre. With his monstrous capitalist footwear, he stamped on the feet of one of those long-nosed nanny-ladies often to be seen in Central Park, guarding the offspring of the aristocracy. Whereupon, affronted by his sudden aggression, she smashed him in the face with her handbag. He fell—dead. By a ruse, pretending qualifications in medicine, I examined him. He was NOT carrying the message."

"Sam Ling," said Lui Ho, in a soft voice. "Tell me, why did Wo Dung fail in this assignment?"

Third-in-command Sam Ling eased his Adam's apple over the collar of his tunic. His drooping moustache moved. His lips stayed still. "Simple reason, Comrade Leader. Unsuccessful assassination alerted enemy agent, who evaded pursuers and had time to secrete or pass on the message before having coronary."

"So ..." sighed Lui Ho. He polished condensed steam off the lenses of his spectacles with the side of his thumb.

27

"Sam Ling, you are promoted to second-in-command." He belched, loudly, then jerked his head at Wo Dung.

"But, beloved Comrade Leader. Our Illustrious Country's choicest ..." began his demoted deputy.

"Elimination," said Lui Ho, firmly. The other spies grabbed Wo Dung, swung him off the ground and forced him, feet-first, into the spin-drier. His pleas became muffled as he disappeared inside, and silent when the door was slammed against his face. Lui Ho nodded. Wo Dung's face stared mistily out through the glass.

Pi Wun Tun, round-faced treasurer of the group, rummaged in his pocket then slotted a handful of coins into the machine.

"It's not only his failure, but also the elaborate imperialistic manner in which he explains it," commented Lui Ho, his head returning to its normal parchment yellow. "He'd make a better poet than spy, and poets are nothing more than drones in the hive of the People's Republic, and flies in the ointment of the Tse Eih Aei. Watch closely, and realise that extensive and honourable labours have their rewards for all, while incompetents and misfits are a capitalist luxury." He pressed the spin-drier starter switch. The machine shuddered. Wo Dung's face righted itself, then jerked upside-down again. The drum gathered speed until the face fattened out and revolved into an indistinguishable blur. Lui Ho twisted the control switch over to the maximum position and smiled. "And how the earnest worker's morale, in our beloved China, will be elevated when they learn that the late Wo Dung lost his life as the result of a revolution in America!"

Lui Ho looked around the small room. "With one less, now all can sit." He opened a large notebook on the table in front of him. "So, we can assume that either the Englishman delivered the message, or that he FAILED to deliver the message."

"So ... so ... so ... so ... so," agreed the other spies.

"Therefore, as the Western pigs have not yet exposed

28

the plan, I have deduced that the message has NOT been passed."

"So ... so ... so ... so ... so."

Lui Ho looked at his five spies. "THEN WHERE IS IT?" He hammered the plywood table with his fist. "Fools, it must be in two of several places. It is either in the museum, OR ... or it is with those long-nose nanny-ladies. If it is in the museum, it'll be like looking for a noodle in a haystack. Not possible to find. But ... if it is with the nanny-ladies, undoubtedly it will reach the running dogs; and this must not happen. So, we must act as follows. We eliminate the nanny-ladies—tonight. You, Fat Choy, will deliver explosive packages to their apartments." Lui Ho paused. "The remainder will attack the museum building with phosphorus grenades. It will be totally destroyed. Attacks are to be made simultaneously from all sides."

"So ... so ... so ... so ..." said four of the spies.

"Possibly not so ..." said the fifth.

"Not *so*, Sam Ling?" asked Lui Ho, coldly. His eyes forced themselves to narrow even more.

"No, Comrade Leader," said Sam Ling. He pictured Lui Ho playing a musical gong in Central Park, while half of New York burned. "Your original idea is much better."

"Original idea?"

Sam Ling crossed his fingers beneath the table. "Yes, Comrade Leader. That idea you mentioned briefly earlier in the meeting—before you were distracted by Wo Dung. You suggested that the nanny-ladies did NOT have the message. You will remember that you asked me if I checked the Englishman's timetable in the museum, and I told you that I had, and that there were just two minutes unaccounted for when the disastrous leadership of Wo Dung permitted the long-nose to escape our vigilance and dispose of the microdot."

"I did?" said Lui Ho.

"Yes," continued Sam Ling. "You perhaps remember suggesting that, although the nanny-ladies might not have the information, they may know of its whereabouts."

"I believe that I begin to remember my saying this."

Sam Ling felt an inward relief. He wished, again, that his government would place the work of espionage in the hands of trained agents, rather than with political enthusiasts.

"You suggested that we should recover the information and return it to our homeland. Thus bringing great credit to this department."

"Yes ..." said Lui Ho. "I remember the last bit quite distinctly. I also remember reading somewhere, and it can only have been in the works of our illustrious leader, that the enemy should always be attacked in its soft underbelly."

Fat Choy raised his eyebrows and looked at Pi Wun Tun.

Lui Ho continued enthusiastically, "So we will attack the soft underbellies of the nanny-ladies." Fat Choy giggled. Lui Ho stared at him coldly. "We will capture the nanny-ladies AND their fat, overfed, delinquent spawn. We'll show them a new way to dry nappies. We'll put them in the spindrier—still on the children. Twenty minutes should be enough. The nanny-ladies will make truthful confessions to alleviate their charges' suffering."

"You certainly said that," said Sam Ling. "But you had one much more brilliant idea."

"Go on," said Lui Ho, "remind me."

"Yes. You said that we should remember the hated, imperialistic times in our beloved Motherland when the bloated families of the white devils who exploited us had such nanny-ladies attached to their families. You so wisely recalled that nanny-ladies were not delicate flowers, even though their complexions resembled the orchid. Orchids with pig-skin petals! Remember the whole battalion of Japanese troopers in the Maidok Mountains ... put to flight by one such orchid who resented the commander raping one of the housegirls?"

"She probably desired the girl, herself," grinned Fat Choy.

"No. In times of stress, these strange, childless and husbandless women show an almost fanatical resistance to pressure. They're NOT paper tigers." Sam Ling switched his gaze from Fat Choy to Lui Ho. "You suggested we should follow the nanny-ladies at all times, and keep a very close watch on them. Tap phones ... check conversations. Let them give us the information we need without their even knowing we want it."

"So ..." Lui Ho beamed at his new deputy. "You are quite correct. I did say ALL that. Sam Ling, you will put electronic listening devices in the nanny-ladies' apartments. You will bug all places where they may talk. And you will arrange a watch on them. EVERY MINUTE OF THE DAY AND NIGHT. Understand?"

"Exactly, Comrade Leader," said Sam Ling. "A most sagacious order."

"So ... so ... so ... so," breathed the other spies.

*   *   *

Hettie's shelves of teddy-bears frowned down at her, accusingly. Their eyes followed her as she stamped through her apartment to the bedroom. She unclipped her pocket-watch and laid it on the bedside table. It ticked, "Room thirteen ... room thirteen ... room thirteen."

She unbuttoned her apron, snicked off a bunch of safety pins and dropped them in a box on the dresser, then opened the linen basket. The lid squeaked ... "world security ... world security."

She sat on the edge of the bed, eased off her shoes and rubbed her feet. She reached down and switched on the air conditioning. The fan gathered speed. "Don't trust anyone ... don't trust anyone ... don't trust ... don't trust ... don't ... don't ... don't ..." Hettie leant against the bed head. It grated a soft "vital ... important ... vital ... important."

She put her hands over her ears, and pushed her stubby fingers into her grey hair.

31

"Och! Dammit, Maister Quincey," she said, "why could-nae you remember what we taught you—always to look where you were going?"

She stretched for the telephone at the side of the bed.

*   *   *

Emily patted nine-month-old Lindon's behind. He lay across her knee, face downwards, his eyes blinking in antici-pation of the thumping. But he didn't cry. The heavy handling gave him a feeling of security. He was gurgling, breathlessly. Emily swung him upright, until he was stand-ing on her knees. She jiggled him. Lindon burped as his stomach muscles sagged. "There you are, then," said Emily. "There you are. All nice and clean. All bathed and pow-dered." She leant forward and sniffed him. "Beautiful," she exclaimed, smiling. She got up and lowered him into his cot.

Outside, in the day-nursery, Lindon's twelve-year-old sister, Dagmar, pulled a face at her elder brother, Carl. "You shouldn't do that to nanny. It's mean and nasty."

"She's senile," he growled. "She's worse than the rest of them. 'You can't do this, Master Carl, you can't do that. It's not the way to behave, Master Carl. You've GOT to be a gentleman, Master Carl.' Hell. I've had it for all my life. I'm fifteen, now. I'm too old for it, and, anyway, it's im-portant for me to go out tonight."

"YOU'VE got a date," teased Dagmar. "Sure, that's what it is. You've got a date with a chick."

"Dry up," snarled Carl. "Go and watch the boob tube if you don't want to help."

"But suppose it hurts her?"

Carl sighed. "It won't. It's quite okay. Everybody at school uses it."

"It's very naughty, but if I help, can I come out with you?"

"Hell, no," scowled Carl. "Tell you what, though. Help

and I'll give you a dollar. You can go out on your own."

"Okay," smiled Dagmar. "How're you going to get her to smoke it?"

"I'm not," said Carl. He scraped the small brown block of resin with the edge of his penknife. "I'm going to mix it with her ice-cream. She'll never notice. It's choc-ice."

Dagmar giggled. "Nanny's going to pot," she laughed.

Carl grinned, and grated more resin into his palm. "That'll do fine," he said, and disappeared into the kitchen.

"Time for bed. Time for bed," warbled Emily, walking into the room, white towels draped over each arm, and her hair standing out from her head like pipe-cleaners. "Come along now, you two. Baths and bed."

"Aw, nanny, I'm fifteen. Can't I stay up a little longer?"

"Time for bed, sleepy head," sang Emily. "Early to bed, early to rise."

Dagmar glanced at Carl and giggled.

"Oh, all right," he said, and winked at his sister.

Emily tidied their rooms while they showered and changed into their night clothes. "Supper," she called. "It's on the table."

The two children appeared in their robes.

"Will you have something to eat with us tonight, please, nanny?"

"I'm not hungry just yet," said Emily.

"Please, Nanny Emily," pleaded Dagmar. "We miss you so much when we go to bed. Please stay and have some supper with us."

"I bought you an ice-cream, specially," said Carl.

"Well ..." said Emily, touched by the unexpected generosity. "Well, all right. Just this once, mind. Special treat. Nanny for supper." She sat down at the table. Carl went back into the kitchen and returned a second later with a large chocolate ice-cream on a saucer.

"Here you are, nanny."

"Ummmmm. It looks delicious, Master Carl. It's very kind of you to think of your old nanny." The children looked at each other and stuck their noses into their cups of milk. Emily spooned the ice-cream into her mouth. When she had finished she dabbed her lips with a napkin. "That was lovely. Thank you both, very much. Now ... off you go to bed."

She tucked Dagmar under the soft blankets, kissed her goodnight and pulled the bedroom door closed behind her. She knocked on Carl's door and called, "Sleep tight." She frowned slightly as he laughed.

The children's day nursery appeared to be growing larger. It now seemed a long way from the table to the nursery kitchen door. Emily collected the supper dishes. They felt very light. She wondered if the maid had substituted plastic dishes for the porcelain ones. She took a step towards the kitchen and nearly fell. Her feet seemed to spring on the carpet, almost as though it was soft, rubber sponge.

She put the dishes in the sink. The last cup dropped from her hand. Amazed, she watched it descend, in slow motion, into the sink. It floated down like a feather. She was quite startled when it shattered on impact, the pieces curling away beneath the washing bowl.

"The heat ..." said Emily to herself. She fanned herself with her pince-nez as she walked towards her own apartment. Her feet dangled in the air. She had to struggle consciously to get them on the ground. She pushed open the door of her room and struggled in, puffing. The flowers on her wallpaper stood out three dimensionally. She blinked.

"Aaaaah ... eeeee ... aaaaaaaah ... eeee ... aaaaaaah," roared her parrot, Tarzan, throwing himself, triumphantly naked, from the bars of his cage to his swing. He waited for Emily's gentle scolding at the sight of the tangle of wool on the cage bottom.

She felt in her handbag, swaying slightly, then produced his new waistcoat. She staggered a couple of steps towards the cage, brandishing the knitting at him. "Naughty, naughty Tarzan. But Nanny's going to stop you, this time." She eyed the interknotted stitches with difficulty, then opened the cage door. Tarzan climbed on to her arm and offered his head to be scratched. "No time, no time," shrilled Emily, wriggling him into the new waistcoat. She pushed his wings through the miniature armholes. The bird seemed to grow heavier. Emily felt she was lifting a bucket of wet sand. She steered Tarzan towards the cage. He fluttered, angrily. Then hopped back in. He climbed laboriously up on to his perch and contemplated his latest woolly conundrum. Emily draped his cage with a piece of maroon towelling. Tarzan gave a final, deafening, ape-man yodel, and settled down for the night.

"Whee," said Emily. She felt suddenly gay. She decided to sing, then stopped herself. Nannies don't sing when their children have just been put to bed, she reminded herself. She switched on her transistor radio. It was no use, she just HAD to sing ... No, she just HAD to FLY. Yes, that was it ... she had to FLY. She wondered what would happen if she jumped up and down on the bed. She scrambled on to the patchwork coverlet and jigged on her feet, waving her arms, like wings.

"What's she doing?" asked Dagmar. Carl replied without removing his eye from Nanny Emily's keyhole.

"She's doing a trampoline act on her bed."

"Let me see. Let me see," demanded Dagmar. Carl pushed her away.

"And she's singing. Her face is VERY red. She's really turned on."

"I hope she doesn't have a heart attack."

"Hell, no, she's just doing her own thing. She'll cool off and sleep. She's just enjoying herself."

Emily watched a small green dinosaur scurry across the floor. It began to climb up the wallpaper. She stretched out a gentle hand, to pat its rump. Startled, it ducked behind the wallpaper flowers. Emily smiled, happily.

Her telephone rang. Emily reached out a nine-foot long arm and picked it up.

"Hello, hello," said a Scots accent. "Hello ... Emily?"

Emily wondered, momentarily, how the telephone came to

35

know her name. She liked its musical voice. She decided to sing her reply.

"It's me-e-e-e. It's me, it's me," she trilled to the tune of the Blue Danube.

She conducted her singing by waving the telephone in front of her. The Scots metallic voice spoke to her from mid-air. "For God's sake, woman. It's Hettie here."

"Hello, Hettie Here," sang Emily. She pushed the earpiece into her spiky hair. What a coincidence, she thought that the telephone should have the same Christian name as her friend.

"We want to talk to you," said the voice. "It's about that dinosaur in the museum."

Emily took the telephone away from her ear and examined it. The round 'O' of the mouthpiece looked startled. She grinned. "There's a dinosaur here, too," she told the mouthpiece, confidentially. "He's very friendly. He just ran up the wall."

"What? Where?" demanded the telephone. "Have you been drinking?"

Emily raised her eyebrows. She wasn't sure she liked telephones that were so impertinent.

"That message in the museum," said the instrument. "We've GOT to find it somehow."

"Then why tell me," said Emily. "I'm sure there are plenty of other telephones who would like to know. There are several kiosks in the museum. Tell THEM about it."

"Holy haggis," said the telephone, in an exasperated tone. "One of us must be going mad. I rang because I hoped you might have some ideas."

"Well, of course," Emily replied. She saw the dinosaur leap off the wallpaper and burrow its way under the bedclothes beside her. She turned to watch it.

"Then what do we do?" asked the telephone.

"We take it home with us," said Emily. "They're very affectionate, really. I think they're just misunderstood."

"Take what home?"

36

"The dinosaur, of course," said Emily. "We take it out of the museum. We rescue it. All dinosaurs must be rescued."

"You mean we steal it?"

"If we talk to it nicely, it'll probably follow us."

"There's no need to be so sarcastic, woman. You think we should take the thing out of the museum so's we can examine it in detail?"

"Exactly that, or something like it," said Emily. The green dinosaur was butting her to gain her attention. "We take it away with us. It's quite tame."

"But it's over sixty feet long," said Hettie.

"No matter how big they are, they're still friendly." Emily began to hum softly to the dinosaur, now curled on her lap.

"There's something wrong with the line, it makes you sound strange," said Hettie. "We'll think about your idea, though. Maybe we could do something like that. We'll talk about it tomorrow. Goodnight."

The telephone clicked into silence. Emily dangled it by its cord for a few moments, then lowered it to the ground. The small dinosaur butted her again, and wriggled its tail in reptilian ecstasy. She scratched its scaly stomach. She suddenly felt very sleepy.

"She's gone off," said Carl to his sister. "I told you she would. I'm going to slip out now."

Dagmar looked worried. "What about her teeth?" she asked. "Nanny always takes them out when she goes to bed. Shouldn't we get them out for her? Maybe she'll choke."

*   *   *

Una viewed television every night of the week, except on her night off. Then she went to the cinema. Tonight she sat in her armchair and watched Marlon Brando kissing his screen mistress. She sighed, and wondered for the millionth time what it felt like to be kissed by a man. The thought made her sneeze. She sighed again. A lot of people were allergic to something—cat's fur, pollen, paint, alcohol. Una

37

was allergic to males. Any sort of males, human or animal. And so, as Nanny Nesbitt, her work was restricted to female children only.

Una was thirty-eight—age and bust. Fate made her attractive to men. But, sadly, made men unattractive to Una. She experienced all the normal feelings, but could never follow them through. A man had only to move in on her and she would sneeze violently. If touched, she came out in a rash. Once, when she was eighteen, a boy had started to kiss her. Regretfully, she'd fainted. She'd tried romances by telephone, even pen pals. They only made her more frustrated..

Brando kissed the girl again. Una watched, her lips slightly apart, as his hands pummelled the girl's body.

Una thought of men. She thought of the 25th Earl. She hadn't met him, but she remembered Melissa's description. He sounded handsome. Such a pity he should have died so young. She tried to imagine herself in Hettie's place and wondered how she'd have felt if it had happened to her. Just terrible. Now there was the problem of the message. She wondered why it was so important.

"I'll love you ... forever ... maybe," mumbled Brando. He swung his leg over his motorcycle and roared away. Una sighed again, then sneezed.

*   *   *

"Stand up," said twenty-two-year-old Nanny Melissa, severely. "How do you expect me to soap you while you're playing with that boat?"

Randall Andrew Jerome the Fourth splashed noisily. He submerged himself until his eye was at bathwater level, then he sighted along his navel, through the steam, at the destroyer, which was just visible against the green marble end of the sunken bath. He torpedoed the warship with his big toe.

A hard, sharp-nailed finger poked his stomach.

"Master Randall," threatened Melissa St. Clair.

Randall stood. His red-haired nanny sponged him. She had gentle fingers, most of the time. He held his arms up. She soaped his armpits, then his chest and back.

She splashed water on his thighs. He heard her sudding the sponge. He looked up at the ceiling and whistled. It was hard to stay in tune while she lathered his thighs, but concentration on the music helped. As usual, he went off key at the critical moment.

"Wash off the soap," ordered Melissa. Her green eyes were determined.

Randall sat down. She swilled hot water over him.

"Now, out you get and dry yourself while I have a quick shower. Okay, darling?"

He nodded.

Randall Andrew Jerome the Fourth climbed out of the bath. He was tall, good-looking, and only twenty-six years old—the playboy heir to a multi-million dollar fortune. His father, always travelling, always busy extending his financial empire, relied on him to control the East Coast section.

Randy'd had British nannies ever since he was a baby. His father had placed a standing order with a domestic employment agency, and another with his bank, to meet the nannies' salaries. The orders had never been rescinded. Jerome Senior had forgotten them, and Jerome Junior preferred not to remind him. For, as Randy grew older, his nannies became younger and prettier. Melissa, he decided, was perfect.

"Bedtime," said Melissa, sharply, when she returned from the shower. "At once, Master Randall."

Randy grinned, and continued pouring himself a drink.

"Now," insisted Melissa. "Or I shall be very angry."

Randy poured another glass and handed it to her. She smiled at him, and put the glass on the bedside table.

"Bed," she said, again.

"Okay," said Randy. "Okay, you win."

"You know the rules," said Melissa.

Randy unbelted his robe and hung it over the foot of the bed. Melissa tutted and carried it to the hook behind the door. Randy climbed into the bed and pulled the sheets up under his chin. Melissa tucked them firmly around him. Then she kissed him quickly on the forehead.

"Goodnight, Master Randall," she said.

"Goodnight, nanny," replied Randy. He waited until she stood back from the bed, then he sat upright. "Thank God for that," he said, reaching for his drink. "Don't you think we could do away with all this nonsense now, this ... charade? I mean, we've been sleeping together for months."

"An agreement's an agreement," said Melissa, picking up her drink and taking a sip. "I'm a nanny until I'm off duty —and that's after I've put you to bed and kissed you goodnight. Then, I'm Melissa."

"But we're getting married soon," persisted Randy.

"And that's when I'll stop being a nanny," smiled Melissa.

Randy climbed out of bed and pulled her towards him. He unbuttoned the front of her housecoat, and held the two sides apart. He looked at her flat stomach, and small, firm breasts.

"You're a very beautiful nanny," he said.

Melissa pouted. "I'm not," she replied. "I'm not a nanny now. I'm just Melissa."

Randy slid the coat off her shoulders. He kissed her. He ran his hands down her back until they rested on the curve of her buttocks. Her thighs pressed against him.

"Take those nasty pyjama things off now, darling," whispered Melissa.

"You only just made me put them on," said Randy.

"Not me. It was Nanny."

"Oh, yes, I forgot." Randy let her undress him. "You know, I guess I like you better as Melissa. You're hands are gentler and more interesting." He pulled her down on to the bed. "Oh, and I've got a complaint."

Melissa's brow furrowed.

"Only a small one," added Randy, quickly. "The talcum

powder. Couldn't we make it some male powder instead of that baby stuff?"

Melissa's fingers moved through the hair on Randy's chest until they reached his navel. She stirred it gently, then slid her hand further downwards.

"Make me a tiger. Make me a tiger and be fierce," she whispered.

"Too hot," replied Randy.

Melissa drew her fingers up the inside of his thigh. Randy felt hotter.

"Make me a tiger, darling. Please."

Randy rolled off the bed and grabbed the skin rug on the floor. He wrapped it over his back, the snarling head resting on his shoulder. He crouched and growled.

Melissa cringed. "More, more," she said, softly.

Randy's tiger prowled on its hands and knees a little nearer.

"Frighten me some more."

He roared and leapt. Melissa screamed as the rug-covered Randy landed on top of her. He bit her, wildly. His hands grasped and clawed her breasts, stomach and back. He kissed her wetly. His teeth nipped her. She writhed and shuddered with excitement.

"Now," whispered Melissa.

"You're doing it again, honey."

"What?" breathed Melissa.

"You're burping me," belched Randy.

*　　*　　*

Putney Willett lolled against the imitation white marble fireplace. The electric glow of the plastic coal reflected gold on his tuxedo. He stretched an arm along the mantelpiece, just as he'd seen in the Bourbon advertisements in *Esquire* ... it was elegant. He was an expert, he knew, in posing. He ought to be, he told himself. He spent far more time practising in front of a mirror than any film or stage actor. He was a diplomat.

"We're going out in a minute, nanny," said Putney Willett, gaily. "Off on the town again. Got to keep up with the social engagements, you know. Yugoslavs tonight." He smoothed his moustache with a long forefinger. "Hey ... hey, now. How's that little dolly of mine been today? A big handful, just like her mommy, I'll bet."

Susanne nodded. "She's just gone off to thleep."

"Sleep, eh? Tired out, I guess. Mind if I go have a look at her, nanny? Mind if I go look at my little darling?"

"By all means, sir." She tried to remember when he had last seen baby Charlotte awake. It certainly wasn't during the past two months.

"Ready, Putney?" demanded a sharp voice.

Mrs. Willett swung into the lounge, a white mink stole over the shoulders of her silk evening gown. "Hell ... where's that darned man gone now? Oh, nanny, where's Mister Willett hidden himself?"

"The nursery, madam," said Susanne.

"Oh, God, that man!" scowled Mrs. Willett. "He will go and play whenever we have something important to do. Really, nanny ... you shouldn't have let him. We're always late for everything." She turned to the mirror over the fireplace and checked her make-up. She watched her husband walk back into the room. "Ah! There you are. Let me have a look at you. Thought so," she said, triumphantly. "Bow's crooked. God, you men! Why don't you get yourself ready, instead of wasting time in the nursery. Turn round, let me see your back." She dusted off imaginary specks. "Come along, we'll be late as usual." She led the way out of the room.

Putney Willett turned back at the door. "Fix yourself a gin-sling, nanny. Get high or something. G'night."

"Put ... ney ..." called Mrs. Willett.

"Nanny ... Nanny ... Nanny." Susanne mimicked her employers' voices, as she heard the front door slam behind them. Why did they have to keep calling her that? It made her feel so old, like Emily and Hettie. And she was only seventeen. Sometimes she wished she worked in a boutique or something. Nannying seemed to be something for older people. She pulled the white starched band off her head, tugging out the pins and shaking her hair down on to her shoulders. She scratched her scalp where the band had made it itch. She walked into her room and pulled off her uniform.

It was still light outside. She walked to the window, opened it and leant out to watch the city below. It was a warm evening. A light flickered on her face. She looked up. A boy, in an apartment across the street, flashed a mirror in the last of the evening sunlight. He disappeared, and returned a few moments later with a large board. It said "Saturday?"

Susanne found the lid of a shoebox and scrawled a reply with her lipstick. "Yes," she held up. The boy waved and vanished into his room. Susanne smiled. She spent most of her off-duty evenings with the boy across the road. And when she was lonely and the sun was in the right direction, she could flash a mirror at him, too. Or, if it was dark, they waved flashlights at each other. They'd even considered learning morse code. It seemed a lot more romantic than telephone calls. He was eighteen, and wanted to be an artist. She knew the other nannies wouldn't approve. Hettie thought that artists were just parasites—that was, unless they were successful. Susanne wondered how an artist could be successful, if he didn't start somewhere?

Maybe his father being a Wall Street stockbroker was the right start.

3

Hettie's white cap bobbed gently in time to the joggling of her foot on the axle of the baby carriage. She folded her arms and watched a cluster of squirrels scatter away from a small black spaniel that lolloped after them. The nannies were sitting on their usual bench in Central Park.

Emily's knitting needles clattered. She finished an uneven row, and scratched her head with the point of the empty needle. She must have been very tired the previous night, she thought. She couldn't even remember going to bed. And this morning the bright colours of her knitting jarred her eyes.

Hettie stopped her carriage-joggling and leant towards the old nanny. "That idea of yours about the dinosaur," she whispered. "Do you really think we could do it?"

"What idea of mine?" asked Emily, starting the next line of Tarzan's newest waistcoat.

"You remember, last night ... on the telephone. You suggested we should steal it."

"STEAL it?" shrieked Emily, scrutinising her from over the top of her pince-nez. The three nannies sitting on her far side looked round, startled.

"Shhhhhh," whispered Hettie. "We thought about it afterwards ... All night. Do you think we could?"

Emily tried to recall the conversation. She couldn't. But she remembered finding the receiver lying on the rug beside her bed this morning. She decided she must have answered the phone while half asleep.

Hettie gave her no time to consider a suitable reply. "We ken there are a lot of problems," she continued. "But then we thought of people like Clive, in India, and Mungo

44

Park, in Africa. They faced immense problems, but they succeeded. Nothing's impossible, and we're doing it for our country. We HAVE to get that message to the queen. If we sent her ALL the bones, she'd know where to look. She receives secret messages all the time."

"But usually by radio, or in documents," said Emily. "I doubt if she's ever had one yet in a dinosaur. Anyway, how do we get the bones to her, EVEN if we do manage to steal them?"

"Post them in parcels marked 'unsolicited gifts', of course. Take it from us, the Customs wouldn't dare to tamper with a present for Her Majesty."

"It'll cost hundreds of pounds," said Emily. "Hundreds and hundreds of pounds."

"It'll cost about three hundred, providing we dinnae send it by airmail. We've got a bit of money put by and we can use some of that. It's the least we can do for Maister Quincey."

"The late 25th Earl," corrected Emily. Hettie nodded.

*   *   *

William floated an empty ice-cream carton on the water of the fountain. The light breeze caught it and blew it out towards the centre. He climbed on to the low wall and reached outwards.

"Don't ..." came Nanny Hettie's voice from the Central Park restaurant behind him. William lowered himself down to the path again and searched for a stone to throw at the carton.

"Maister William," called Hettie. "Stop dragging your feet, laddie. Go and play on the grass."

The five nannies sheltered from the hot afternoon sun, under the blue and red umbrellas of the café. They sipped iced wine in fruit juice. It was an extravagance by normal standards, but Hettie thought it was in keeping with the conspiratorial occasion.

"We've GOT to do something," continued Hettie, when she had made certain that Master William wasn't going to drown himself. "Both Emily and myself are too old to do it on our own. We need your help. You all know we wouldn't ask if it was just for us. This is something we have to do to help our dear country. Maybe the whole world, too. You do understand, don't you? Will you help?"

The three younger nannies looked at her, then at each other.

"Well?" asked Hettie.

"I'd be proud to," said Susanne. "I don't even mind if they thoot me, though I don't think I'd like having a black bag thtuck over my head."

"You can count me in, too." Melissa looked at Hettie. "But I hate to think what Randy will say if we should get caught."

"There IS a risk," added Una. "We COULD get caught. And I suppose we'd be charged with theft. It's a serious offence to rob a museum."

"Aye," said Hettie. "It is that. But we're quite sure the risk's worth taking. And, of course, from a moral point of view, we know we aren't stealing, just borrowing. In fact, we'll include a note to Her Majesty, asking her to return the bones to the museum when she's found the secret message." She paused.

"So we can count on your help? ALL of you—without reservation?" Hettie watched her friends' faces, anxiously, as they smiled their assent. "Good. We knew we could depend on you. And here's how we can do it. We remember the late king. He loved children, and Christmas. And he used to do conjuring tricks. We remember one he did with a glass under a silk handkerchief. He used to wave a wee wand at it, and the glass would disappear. We had a look in his conjuring box afterwards. There was a wire shape fitted in the handkerchief that only looked like a glass. He used to take the real glass away beforehand and nobody noticed."

"We'll need more than a wee wand for a dirty great dinothaur," said Susanne.

"Hush," continued Hettie. "You remember last year, when the museum people painted round the elephant display? They covered the animals with big canvas sheets."

"I remember Master Carl tipping over a can of their paint," muttered Emily.

"Aye. Well, we thought a bit more. And maybe this is the answer. If we could get the museum people to paint the dinosaur hall, they'll have to cover the beastie with canvas sheets, like the elephants. Then we'll be able to get underneath and dismantle the skeleton and take it away piecemeal —WITHOUT anyone noticing, because the canvas will still be kept in shape by the iron frame. It may mean camping under the canvas till we've finished. But we dinnae see that as a problem. It'll take the painters the best part of a week to do that room."

"But this is urgent. How are we going to persuade a museum to paint one of its halls, and in a matter of days?" asked Una. "It's quite impossible."

"That's the problem we haven't been able to solve yet," admitted Hettie.

Susanne grinned. "I'll bet I could get them to paint it quickly," she said. "We could deface a piece of it. You know, write thomething awful. They'd paint that out thoon enough."

"Vandalism," growled Hettie. "Typical younger generation suggestion. Always sitting down for things. Rioting. Writing on walls. Completely irresponsible."

"Maybe it's not such a bad idea," suggested Melissa. "Perhaps we COULD write something that wasn't TOO rude. Just rude enough to be lightly painted over. After all, it ..."

Emily's voice broke in. "Wait a minute. I've just had a thought." She looked at them with a smile of triumph on her lips. "I think I know a way we can get them to paint the ceiling. AND we don't have to persuade them to. In fact, we tell them NOT to paint anything."

"How?" asked Susanne. "How do we get thomeone to do thomething by telling them not to?"

"For a children's nurse, you surprise me," said Emily. "What happens if you tell a child not to touch an electric switch?"

"They touch it," said Susanne.

"Precisely."

"But this is a museum, not a kindergarten."

"Ah," Emily said, softly. "But it depends on WHAT we tell the museum. Hettie, I shall want to borrow your royal testimonial, or one of your special letters, to make it work."

The other nannies looked surprised. The references and letters Hettie had received from the queen at the end of her service with the royal family were guarded like moonrock. They had only been allowed to see them after much pleading. A quick glimpse each, a warning not to touch them, and Hettie had replaced them in their envelopes, and the envelopes back into her small cash box.

"My ROYAL testimonials?"

"Or a letter. It'll be quite safe, I promise. I only want it for a couple of hours tomorrow morning. I'll give it back to you in the afternoon." Emily leant forward and whispered. "I want to do something quite naughty. I want to copy the palace notepaper."

"Och, no ..." gasped Hettie. The other nannies looked horrified.

"Yes," Emily whispered. "I need it to write a letter to the museum. And I'm quite sure Her Majesty wouldn't object if she knew the reason."

*　　　*　　　*

It was early evening in the sewer headquarters, the time that the Tse Eih Aei spies hated most of all. Between seven and eight was generally shower time for guests at the Plaza Hotel, and hot perfumed steam penetrated the small room, turning it into an uncomfortable Turkish bath. The

48

Chinese agents, wearing only loincloths, were *still* sweating.

"So ..." Lui Ho hissed through the scented fog. "Sam Ling, what information have your electronic listening devices revealed?"

"Plenty of good information," said Sam Ling, rubbing perspiration into his shoulders. He wondered if, after making his report, he should ask Fat Choy to give him a massage.

Pi Wun Tun sat on the edge of his bunk, swinging his feet. Sam Ling's dedicated efficiency made him nervous. And the way he managed to make his Mongolian moustache smile, while his thin lips remained perfectly horizontal, didn't help, either. Now that he'd become Lui Ho's second-in-command, Sam Ling had ceased to be as friendly as he'd been. Pi Wun Tun felt that Sam Ling was almost as dangerous an ally as he could be as an enemy.

Lui Ho mopped his scalp with a towel, and fanned himself with his copy of the Chairman Mao's Quotations. "Go on, then. Tell me what you have discovered."

"The ladies are nanny-ladies," began Sam Ling.

"We knew that."

"Yes, we knew that. But, most important, and something we didn't suspect, was that the red-faced one, who looks like an overgrown tomato fruit, was nanny-lady to the British agent who died."

"Ah ... so ... so ... so ... so ..." said the five other spies, softly.

"She killed him. He did not have that capitalist sickness—heart attack, known to us as American blight. She broke his suicide capsule." Sam Ling grinned. The other spies giggled.

"So ... ?"

"The agent had time to speak to his nanny-lady before he died. He did NOT hand over the message. But he told his nanny-lady where it is hidden."

"Where?" breathed Lui Ho.

"As you suspected, chief. In the museum. In the dinosaur."

"Marvellous!" exclaimed Lui Ho. "Who would have thought of looking in a dinosaur? Not even I. Er ... what is a dinosaur?"

"A dragon," said Sam Ling. "The greatest monster that ever left the moon to walk this earth."

"Aieee ... a dragon monster," chorused the other spies.

Lui Ho blanched. "Foolishness. Imperialistic poppycock. There are no such things as dragons. Monsters, perhaps. But not dragons." Lui Ho stood and pointed towards the poster on the wall. "It is written there—in the beautiful words of beloved Mao Tse-tung." He read the wording in full. "People of the World Unite and defeat the U.S. aggressors and all their running dogs! People of the World, be courageous, dare to fight, defy difficulties, and advance wave upon wave. Then the whole world will belong to the people. Monsters of all kinds shall be destroyed."

The spies cheered, enthusiastically. Lui Ho folded his arms across his chest. "There it is, written by Mao Tse-tung. Monsters of all kinds shall be destroyed. See how the words of the beloved Chairman cover all eventualities. We can safely assume that dragons do NOT exist, otherwise he would have specifically mentioned them."

"The monster is a dragon," said Sam Ling. "I have seen it."

"Do not provoke my anger, you bourgeois revisionist," roared Lui Ho, his scalp working its way through the full spectrum of colours. "Do you call our beloved Mao a liar?"

Sam Ling backed away, hurriedly. "No, no. Of course not. The dragon must be an American capitalist hoax. Something to mislead the people. It is a fake, perhaps. Yes, definitely. The dragon in the museum is a fake. Nevertheless, the information is hidden in the dragon."

"In the likeness of the dragon," hissed Lui Ho, his head beginning to regain its normal colouring. "Then we must destroy it. Tonight, we will blow open the doors of the museum, advancing wave upon wave, as our revered leader has written. We will then machine-gun the guards, and take away the paper dragon."

"The paper dragon is cunningly constructed of bone," said Sam Ling, quietly. "In all probability, it weighs ten thousand pounds. But, Comrade Leader, I have a further suggestion based on information I have gathered." He paused. "On your orders, of course."

"Take care that you do not suggest yourself into oblivion," warned Lui Ho. "Also at my orders."

Sam Ling blinked away a bead of perspiration running onto his left eyelid, crossed his fingers behind his back, and continued. "I am basing this suggestion on an idea of your own, Comrade Leader. You are so filled with wondrous ideas that we, of lesser thinking capacity, have difficulty in remembering all the great things you devise. But, by racking my poor memory, I remember something you said . . . 'let the enemy work for us'." Sam Ling began to wonder if he'd get a permanent twist in his crossed fingers. "The nanny-ladies are themselves planning to take the dragon . . . er, the fake dragon, out of the museum. I believe you will want us to let them succeed in their plan. And you will want us to let them take it away to the hiding place they will have prepared. And THEN we'll take it from them. This idea of yours would seem less risk for us."

"And why should THEY take the fake dragon?" asked Lui Ho.

"Because, in their amateurish way, they have already searched it for the message. And I suspect the agent hid a microdot in a crack in one of the bones, and perhaps even plastered over it."

"So . . ." said Lui Ho. "Yes, you are correct, my idea is a sound one . . . based . . ." he added swiftly, "based on the thinking of our beloved leader, Chairman Mao Tsetung." He saluted the two portraits on the shelf. "We will let the enemy help us. They will steal the fake dragon. We will take it from them and examine it at our leisure."

"Send it back to China," corrected Sam Ling.

"Yes, as I was saying, we'll examine it at our leisure, in China."

*　　*　　*

For an ice-cream barrow, it was extremely hot inside. Sam Ling sat, jammed between the two ice-cream cylinders, his legs hunched beneath him. He was adjusting the tape-recorder monitoring the nannies' conversation. The cart bumped and juddered as Chou-Tan pushed it towards the nannies, sitting on their usual park bench.

Sam Ling breathed out and tried to make himself smaller, so that he could peer out through the holes drilled in the front of the barrow. He twisted his arm above him and rapped on the low roof.

Chou-Tan lifted the lid of the front ice-cream container and squinted down. "Yes?"

"Not too near," ordered Sam Ling, looking up through the dummy cylinder, and getting a distorted underneath view of Chou-Tan's artificial Italian moustache. "And try to stop the wheels squeaking. They're being picked up on the recorder."

Chou-Tan nodded at the container.

Sam Ling pulled on his earphones. Not that he needed them for checking the tapes. It was just that the genuine container of ice-cream was giving his left ear frostbite, while the rest of him was being pot-roasted in the confined space. He could hear the nannies' voices clearly transmitted from the small listening bug drilled into the back of the park bench.

"They're amazing," he heard one of them say. It was Una, she held a sheet of white paper up to the sunlight. "The only difference is the watermark."

"I couldn't manage that," replied Emily. "Otherwise, I don't think it's a bad match for a photocopy."

"Let us see." Hettie reached out a hand for the reproduction Buckingham Palace notepaper. It was really VERY good. It took a close examination to spot the difference. There were no signs that it was anything but a genuine piece of Buckingham Palace notepaper bearing the royal signature.

"Here's the one I'm sending." Emily pulled an envelope from her handbag and extracted another sheet of notepaper. This had a letter, neatly typed, above the royal name.

"I'll read it to you," she said. "It's addressed to the Director of the Museum." She paused and took a deep breath. "Dear Sir . . . this is a request on behalf of our eldest son, who is, as you may know, a student of archaeology. He wishes to examine the specimens in your famous Early Dinosaur Hall—as they are among the finest available in the world. He will . . ."

Emily panted for a few seconds, then began again.

"He will arrive in New York in about fourteen days' time and will travel incognito. It is unnecessary for you to make any special arrangements, like redecorating the Early Dinosaur Hall or removing the direction signs to the ladies' lavatories, or deodorising the drains. Charles is well travelled and knows about things like that. Please just treat him as you would any other Crown Prince.

"We ask only that he be given every help in the pursuit of his studies . . . Yours faithfully . . . There, how's that?"

"Och, that doesnae sound like a royal letter to us," said Hettie. "It's almost sacrilege."

"I composed it most carefully," said Emily, peevishly. "It has to be friendly and chatty, not too formal. Just like an ordinary mother looking after her boy."

"How will that letter make them paint the museum?" asked Una.

"Human nature," replied Emily. "You wait. It'll happen."

She put the letter back in the envelope and sealed it. Twenty minutes later it was in the hands of the U.S. Post Office. The following morning it was opened by the museum director.

"Hmmmm." He handed it back to his secretary. "Check it out with the British Embassy. You never know, might just be right."

By five that evening, it was collected, along with other refuse, by the museum garbage man.

*   *   *

Lui Ho cleared his throat and spat noisily, as the thick steam from the Plaza showers gushed into the Tse Eih Aei headquarters.

"Learn to play the piano," he said, through the fog. "It is written here, in the book."

His spies, relaxing naked or loincloth-clad in their bunks, tried to look wise, and prepared themselves for the inevitable lecture.

"Our beloved Mao writes that, in playing the piano, all ten fingers are in motion; it won't do to move some fingers only, and not others.

"But if all ten fingers press down at once, there is no melody. To produce good music, the ten fingers should move rhythmically and in co-ordination." Lui Ho paused. On his bunk, Fat Choy counted his fingers. He could find only eight, and two thumbs. He suddenly felt sorry for himself. Mao Tse-tung was NEVER wrong. Therefore he, Fat Choy, must be deformed.

"It means that we fingers must work in rhythm," continued Lui Ho. He peered at Sam Ling, whose head was contained in a turban-like bandage. "Two of our fingers were not working rhythmically today, were they? Wounded? Wounded? How does one get oneself wounded in an ice-cream barrow?"

"I was wounded, almost trepanned, by a certain colleague who forgot which was the dummy barrel, and tried to spoon ten cents' worth of my head into a cornet," protested Sam Ling.

"But, Comrade Leader, I made a day's profit of nine

54

dollars, fifty-three cents," said Chou-Tan, proudly.

"Good," replied Lui Ho. "Dollars are always useful. And now . . . play back the recording of the nanny-ladies' meeting."

The spies listened as the tapes spun through the machine. Lui Ho's frown wrinkled back on to his scalp.

"Those strange noises are smackings, and children crying," explained Sam Ling. "And one must remember to ignore the normal domestic conversation. You will readily see that these nanny-ladies lack any form of sophistication in the art of intrigue."

"Will their plan work?" asked Pi Wun Tun. He hoped that no one would suddenly suggest they should all stand to salute Chairman Mao's portraits, as the soft voices of the nannies and the slapping noises had given him an erection.

Sam Ling shook his head in silent reply.

"Then," said Lui Ho. "Tonight we will mount our portable short-range rocket launcher in the bushes of Central Park. We will fire an explosive missile into the museum, in the appropriate gallery, thus necessitating redecoration of that part."

"Not only redecoration, Comrade Leader, but certain rebuilding. And we cannot wait that long." Sam Ling's fingers wound themselves automatically as he went on. "I believe that, earlier, you had ideas which could be put into excellent use at this time."

Lui Ho peered at him from under his straight black eyebrows. "Yes?"

"You suggested, with your usual luminosity, Comrade Leader, that WE should assist the nanny-ladies. You said we should help them, but remain anonymously in the background. They can be helped in many ways."

"As you say," grunted Lui Ho. "I am indeed brilliant, but cursed by such a poor memory. No doubt it could be traced to some inherited imperialistic weakness that will, no doubt, be bred out of future generations."

"A minor fault, Comrade Leader," said Sam Ling, his

fingers relaxing. "Now, here's what you probably suggested . . ."

*　　*　　*

Two full days passed before there were any developments in the nannies' plans. Nothing seemed to be happening. They waited anxiously. Then, on the third morning, an excited Emily arrived at the park bench. She was puffing and out of breath. Her spiky hair stood out around her cap, and her pince-nez were steamed up.

"It worked!" she gasped, happily. "I told you it would work. I've just come from the museum, and they've already started to do something. I saw men carrying lots of steel tubing, and tins of paint and things along the corridors."

Hettie looked at her in disbelief. "Away with you," she said.

"Absolutely honestly," Emily protested. "I swear it. They're going to redecorate that hall."

"Then the museum director must be a wee bit daft," said the Scots nanny. "That letter didnae sound at all as though it was written by Her Majesty."

She noticed Emily's hurt look, and she reached out and patted her arm. "There, we're sorry we didnae completely believe in you. But we're VERY pleased to hear your news. We're sure the 25th Earl would be delighted."

Una smiled at Emily. "People always believe the things they want to believe. The museum man would probably LIKE to be visited by a Crown Prince. THAT'S why he believed the letter."

"Not at all," insisted Emily. "It was because I wrote that letter exactly how I thought Her Majesty would write it. I just imagined myself to be the queen, and a boy's mother, and wrote quite naturally."

"Right, ma bonnies," said Hettie. "Let's not waste any more time. It's enough that Nanny Emily's idea came off. Now we can get down to the real work. Let's away to the

56

museum first, and see what's going on there. Una, it's your turn to look after the bairns while we go in."

*　　*　　*

The nannies stood at the entrance to the hall and watched the men pull a heavy, yellow canvas sheet over the fossilised brontosaurus.

"There," said Emily. "I told you. It's just as I said it would be. We'll watch for a few minutes."

Hettie looked round the hall to familiarise herself with the positioning of the scaffolding.

The hall attendant strolled over to the group.

"Sorry, ladies. You can't come in now. We've got some decorations to restore."

A sly look came over Emily's face. "Are you expecting visitors?" she asked.

"Expecting them?" The man scowled. "Lady, we've just had them. Nearly cost me my job. Some nut squirted Commie peace slogans on the ceiling."

"Paint?" queried Emily.

The man nodded, and pointed. There were several large blotches on the high roof.

"And that ain't all," he growled. "You should read what he wrote on the walls about the president . . ." He turned to show them, then changed his mind. "Guess you'd better go now, ladies. We got work to do. Why not come back in a week's time? You'll be able to see the old bront, then." He winked at Emily. "He ain't going anywhere."

Emily's face was angry. She turned towards Susanne. The young nanny shook her head, violently. "It wathn't me, truly," she whispered, hurriedly. "It'th jutht a horrid cointhidence."

*　　*　　*

"Robert Bruce, General Gordon, Flora Macdonald," said

57

Hettie, when they had joined Una in the park again. "And maybe the MacPhish of Kingussie."

"Who?" asked Melissa.

"Sorry," said Hettie. "We were just thinking of people we'd like to have with us on a raid like this."

"I've heard of most of them," said Susanne. "But who's the MacPhish of whatever-it-was?"

"A relation," said Hettie. She didn't explain that it was her grandfather, a red-bearded giant of a drunkard who needed a whole lorry-load of Glasgow policemen to get him out of the Kingussie Street Arms any night of the week.

Susanne thought of the statue outside the museum. "I'd like to have Theodore Roosevelt with uth. He wath brave, and audacious."

"Not so audacious as you, expecting him to help you rob his own memorial," laughed Una.

"The dear, late king was always my hero," said Emily, nostalgically. "He'd have taken a dinosaur to save England. I can picture him doing it just like the scene on the back of a gold sovereign."

"King George, a saint! How perfectly apt," said Hettie. "And how romantic. He was a REAL gentleman."

"Breeding, my dear," said Emily, brushing down the front of her uniform, then straightening the cushions in her baby carriage.

"Now for some careful planning. We've got to handle this like a military operation," said Hettie. She pictured herself, a clan leader, kilt-clad and armed with a heavy claymore, with her followers on the eve of Culloden. "Over the top we'll go. Trumpets sounding the charge. Horses' hooves thundering. Banners waving in the breeze. Wi' the clans howling their war cries. That's how it'll be."

The four nannies looked at her in amazement. "Well, er, not quite like that," Hettie corrected herself. "We'll be most ladylike, and extremely discreet."

"D'you think we should try thmuggling the bones out under our thkirts?" asked Susanne. "I once heard of a shop-

58

lifter who dressed herself as an expectant lady and filled a thpecial pair of flannel knickers with radio thets. She'd have got away with it, too, but one of them got thwitched on, and the thtore detective heard her giving out a weather forecast."

"Humph," said Emily. "We're not shoplifters. And I've not wasted my time during the last two days. I've already thought of a way of getting the bones out of the museum. I've found a good escape route. I started working on the idea, knowing that my letter was going to make the museum paint that hall."

"But the man in the hall thaid . . ." began Susanne.

"Stuff and nonsense," said Emily. "Perhaps they ARE painting the hall because someone wrote something stupid on the walls. But I KNOW they'd have done it, anyway. I wouldn't be at all surprised if the museum director found he couldn't get permission to decorate the hall for his royal visitor, so he went out and wrote the rude slogans himself, in order to justify the work."

"Quaite," said Una's exaggerately-refined North London voice. She glanced at her watch. "My goodness, it's four fifteen."

Hettie checked her own timepiece. "We'll have to hurry, or we'll miss tea-time. Let's go and have it at the Tavern. And we'll talk more about the plan there." She turned to Emily and whispered, quietly. "Remember, this is our responsibility, Nanny Emily. Partly your plan . . . but our full responsibility. We are still the senior nurse when it comes to making final decisions. Now, kindly explain your plan to us."

Emily nodded.

They parked the perambulators in the tree-shaded open-air café, and sat at a nearby table.

"Tea, everybody?" asked Hettie, as a waitress neared them. "Not, of course, that we'll get REAL tea, anyway. Tea-bag tea, ugh! I hate to think what would have happened if you'd served tea-bag tea to H.R.H. at a Royal Garden Party."

"Coke for me, please," said Susanne.

"Nonsense, girl. Tea . . . or perhaps, as a treat, lemon-tea."

"I want a sixty-foot length of rope," confided Emily, her mind running through the equipment they would be needing.

"Sure, lady," said the waitress, her face bland. "How do you British like it? Grilled, poached, or our speciality, rope suzette?"

Emily stared at the slim girl in her blue nylon dress.

"Just tea, thank you," she said, grandly. She waited until the girl had left them, then she turned to the others. "Providing Nanny Hettie agrees, then I'd like you all to get the night after tomorrow, off. Meanwhile, here's a list of the things that I . . . er, Nanny Hettie and I, want you to get. Melissa, you buy the rope. Sixty feet of mountaineering stuff. Try a sports equipment emporium. Susanne, you get two large adjustable wrenches and two big screwdrivers. And some grocer's sacks and bags. Una, just lanterns, and torches. Four of them. And get spare batteries and bulbs. And Hettie, you and I will buy a lorry."

"Lorry?" exploded Hettie. "Gracious me, and why would we be needing a lorry?"

"To carry the bones, of course," smiled Emily. "And I shall drive."

"You can drive a lorry, Nanny Emily?" Susanne looked at the old lady with surprise.

"I'll have you know, my girl, I drove a caterpillar tractor during the war, on Lord Bramwell's estate. I was responsible for ploughing five acres."

"We heard about that," said Hettie. "At the Land Army Club they said it was the longest furrow ever ploughed. Five acres it may have been, but it was in one straight line. You nearly cut off Devon and Cornwall. One furrow, from Exeter to Barnstaple. They had no electric power in the West Country for a week."

"The throttle jammed," Emily pouted. "I had to wait

60

until the fuel ran out. Anyhow, I've borrowed a book about driving from the library, and tonight I'm going to read it. I'm quite sure that if a mere lorry driver can drive a lorry, so can I."

"Aye, maybe," said Hettie, doubtfully. She looked at her watch, then at the three younger nannies. "Time we were away. Now dinnae forget the things we told you about."

Emily's head wagged so vigorously in agreement that her pince-nez rattled. "Yes, and bring them round to my flat in the morning. You'd better bring some working clothes and gloves, too. It's going to be a dusty job."

*　　*　　*

Click-clack, click-clack, click-clack. Sam Ling peered down over the edge of his bunk, and tried to make out who was playing table-tennis in the evening steam-fog of the Tse Eih Aei headquarters.

"Van in," said Fat Choy's voice. "Where's the ball?"

"In the corner," replied Pi Wun Tun. "You'll have to get it."

Fat Choy groaned, and climbed out of his bunk.

"You two are the laziest sportsmen I've ever met," Sam Ling muttered. "I've never before seen anyone playing ping-pong lying down."

"It's more relaxing," grunted Pi Wun Tun. "And more skilful. One needs complete concentration to maintain accuracy from a prone position."

"Lotus-eaters," said Sam Ling.

The fog swirled as the lift descended into the room, and Lui Ho stepped out. He wafted the mist away from him, flapping his hands. "Is everybody here?" he called.

"All except Nicky Po," answered Sam Ling, swinging his legs over the side of his bunk and dropping to the ground. "He's fishing again."

Lui Ho's eyes glazed. He ran a thin tongue over his lips. "Fish Manchu," he whispered. "Lobster on a perfumed bed of snow-bleached rice. Delicate Pacific squid broiled in its own exotic ink." The spies watched him with sad faces. "Thin slivers of pink shark meat balanced on silver skewers, and roasting over charcoal ..." Lui Ho sighed deeply. "Nicky Po is one true comrade who makes exquisite efforts to fully occupy his time and enhance our deprived diet." Lui Ho made a visible effort to concentrate on Sam Ling's report. "So, Second in Command to myself, what DID you learn today about those female Capitalist lackeys?"

"Our plan worked . . . er, your plan. Pi Wun Tun's efforts in the hall of the fake dragon brought immediate results. The museum authorities have begun their repainting, and the nanny-ladies have started phase two of their operation."

"Excellent. Excellent." Lui Ho rubbed his steam-slippery hands together. "So we act tonight?"

"No, tomorrow, if all goes well."

"Good," smiled Lui Ho. "See that nothing disturbs them at their work. Nothing, absolutely nothing, must go wrong with their plan." He rummaged in his pocket and pulled out his red book. He flicked the pages.

Fat Choy sighed quietly. He wondered if, today, he was going to learn that he had too few toes.

Lui Ho cleared his throat and began to read. "Thousands upon thousands of martyrs have heroically laid down their lives for the people; let us hold their banner high and march ahead along the path crimson with their . . ."

He was interrupted by a splashing, scuffling sound. An effluent-smeared figure staggered in through the mist, dripping eerily, its thigh-boots overflowing. It clutched a wriggling heap of mud in its arms. "Eee-ee-ee-ee," it cried delightedly.

"A devil," gasped Fat Choy, hiding his head under his damp blanket.

Lui Ho squinted through his moist spectacles. "Nicky Po."

"I've caught one . . . I've caught one," shouted the slime-

·covered apparition. "Tonight we will all have the most delectable and exotic repast."

"Holy dung beetles," moaned Lui Ho in horror. "Not another sewer alligator!"

4

The sharply dressed young salesman at Happy Harry's Used Car Lot and Rebuild Emporium flicked a minuscule speck of tobacco ash from the lapel of his shiny mohair, and peered through the one-way inspection window. Two women, children's nurses, he guessed, from their white uniforms and lace-up shoes, were wandering around the truck section. They stopped in front of a yellow, seven-ton, long-wheelbase Dodge. He couldn't believe it. Hardly anyone bought yellow, seven-ton, long-wheelbase Dodges in the condition of that one, especially nannies.

The short, odd-looking one, with the funny glasses and twitching nose, shook her head. The salesman split a match with his thumbnail and began picking his teeth. He saw her indicate a refrigerator truck further down the line. He bit on his piece of wood. Nurses didn't buy refrigerator trucks, either.

He kicked open the shaky door of the timber shack that served as Happy Harry's office, and strolled over to the two women.

"The automobiles are over there, lady." He pointed to the battered rows of hasty repaints that were rusting away discreetly on the other side of the lot. "We got heaps of bargains, repossessions, insurance jobs, low mileage autos—

last you—" he eyed the two women—"last you a lifetime."

"We want a vehicle for carrying things," said the one with the pince-nez. "Not small things, but things a bit bigger than you." She eyed the salesman. "Quite a few things, quite a bit bigger than you, my good man."

The salesman immediately thought of 'Arsenic and Old Lace'.

"You want a hearse?"

"Goodness, of course not," snapped the other woman, in a Scots accent. "We're not carrying dead bodies."

"Well, not actually dead bodies," added the older nurse. "But it has to be quite a big vehicle. And frightfully reliable, too."

"I got a good one here," said the salesman, pointing to a battered green Ford. "Almost brand new inside. Just wants a slight clean-up. A rare model. Only done twenty thousand miles." He thought for a moment. "One careful operator . . . a doctor."

Emily's brows furrowed. "Then the gentleman must have been a witch doctor. It looks as though it was driven here from darkest Africa. How about that one?" She nodded towards a deep blue Chevrolet that looked like a furniture removal van. It had a split and dented fender but otherwise seemed fairly clean. "How much?"

"Three hundred dollars, lady," said the salesman. "Best truck in the lot. Perfect working condition. It's a steal. Broke the guy's heart to get rid of it. He owned a pet shop. Only used it to carry animals and birds. Came in yesterday."

"Start the motor," said Emily, sternly.

The salesman reached in and twisted the key. To his relief, the batteries spun the engine to life. He stepped back.

"First-rate," he said. "Good starter, excellent runner." He looked at the two women. "It carries our usual seven-day guarantee."

"We'll take it," said Hettie. "Show our friend here how it works."

"How it works?" asked the salesman.

64

"Yes. How does it start? And which is the gear lever?"

"You sure you ladies want a truck?"

"We'll pay cash," said Hettie.

"How's that?"

"Cash, man, cash!" repeated Hettie, opening her handbag. She pulled out a roll of notes. The salesman bit his lip. He couldn't remember the last customer of Happy Harry's who'd even had fifty dollars in bills.

"You'll never regret buying this truck, ladies. I'll take you round the block, personally. Make sure you know how it handles."

Minutes later, the truck was back outside Happy Harry's Lot. Emily sat at the huge wheel, joyfully revving the engine, while inside the shack-like office, the salesman was collecting three hundred dollars from Hettie and handing her the vehicle documents in exchange.

The deal completed, they emerged together through the door.

"Well, good luck, ladies," called the salesman, as Hettie settled herself next to Emily. "Don't forget what I told you —keep her on a tight leash. She's a mile-eater, that one." He grinned as the old nanny trod down on the clutch pedal and crashed into gear. The wheels hopped. Then the truck bounded away.

"We're a wee bittie nervous," confessed Hettie.

"Nervous? Nervous? Nonsense, woman. I'm perfectly competent at driving, now."

"Not about the driving, the bairns." Hettie shuffled herself more comfortably on the passenger seat. "We're just nervous leaving them with Melissa and Susanne. We dinnae feel they've got enough experience to manage so many."

"They will have by the end of the week," promised Emily. "We're all going to have to share each other's children. What better way could they learn?"

"That reminds us," said Hettie. "Last night we had an odd telephone call. A strange voice—very deep for a woman's. Said they were the Comrade Nanny-Ladies'

Replacement Bureau. It's some service we haven't heard of before. Charitable . . . doesn't cost anything. Whenever a nanny needs extra time off, they send a specially-trained nurse as replacement. They said days or nights, for as long as necessary. And it's free."

"Thoroughly untrustworthy, I should think," said Emily.

"Och, of course," nodded Hettie. "As if we'd leave a child of ours with strangers."

Emily was enjoying herself. The truck was big and powerful. She liked sitting high above the other traffic, and she began to understand how bus and lorry drivers felt, on their thrones, when they leant out of their cabs and cursed and swore at the other road users.

She glanced at the speedometer. It showed eighteen miles an hour. The transmission was howling for a gear-change. But by the time she'd remembered the correct procedure, had pressed down the clutch pedal and sought the second gear position, the truck's speed had fallen to five miles an hour. Then it jerked, and stalled.

"Why have we stopped?" asked Hettie.

"Adjustments," replied Emily, fiddling with the gear lever, and then re-positioning her pince-nez.

She remembered the salesman's instructions, pulled the gear stick into neutral, turned the ignition key and started all over again. This time she changed gear successfully. Three times! There was the sound of a siren alongside them. A motorcycle patrolman waved.

"He recognises us," said Emily.

Hettie sniffed and wriggled her shoulders primly. "We don't think we recognise him."

The speedcop shouted something at them. He swerved his machine in front of the truck, missing them by inches, then slowed down.

"That was dangerous," said Emily. "Do you think he wants to talk to us?"

The Harley Davidson stopped ahead of them. Emily struggled with the gear lever and the brakes. The truck kangarooed to a stop half an inch from the motorcycle's polished rear fender.

The speedcop turned a slightly darker shade of crimson and pulled out his notebook as he walked round to the driver's window.

"Okay, bud," he began, then noticed the two women. "Oh, God . . . Dames. Dames driving trucks!" He leant forward and pulled open the cab door.

"Okay, ladies . . ."

The two women peered down. The cop looked them over.

"Now what's a coupla nice old nurses like you doing driving around like drag-racers?"

They were silent.

"I know," continued the cop. "You was on the way to the hospital. Don't tell me, let me guess. You're Dr. Kildare and you're late for an operation. Well . . ." he paused and began writing in his book. "Well, I gotta message for you . . . sort of a prescription." He licked the end of his pencil and continued writing. "Gotya licence?"

"Er . . . no . . ." said Emily. "Sorry, constable."

"Whadja mean, constable? I'm a cop. You dames foreigners?"

"Most certainly not, laddie," replied Hettie, fiercely. "YOU'RE foreign. WE'RE British."

"Yes British," added Emily. "This lady is a royal nanny. You should be more polite."

"A royal what?" asked the patrolman.

"Nanny—a governess," said Emily.

"An Embassy official?"

"Royal governess," repeated Emily. She polished her pince-nez on a handkerchief and perched them back on her twitching nose.

"We teach manners, my man," said Hettie.

"You claiming diplomatic immunity?" The cop vaguely remembered something unpleasant happening to a friend who'd stopped another foreign driver who turned out to be a Danish prince. He shut his notebook with a slap.

"You got a passport, then? Alien's Registration Card?"

"They're at home," said Emily.

"No identification, eh? No proof of diplomatic immunity?"

"Identification? Proof?" growled Hettie. "We're ladies. And British. Surely, our word's good enough?"

"I gotta have identification," muttered the patrolman. He fished in his breast pocket, and pulled out his warrant card. "Something like this."

Hettie took the card and examined the photograph, then compared it with the patrolman's face. "Very interesting, laddie." She handed it back to him. "All right then, officer. You can go now. And behave yourself."

"Thank you, ma'am," said the cop, automatically. He pushed his warrant card back into his pocket and began to walk to his machine. Then, he hesitated, thought for a second and turned back. "Hey, I'm supposed to be the one who says that."

"Says what?" asked Emily, as she twisted the ignition key.

"You can go now," he repeated.

"Why, thank you, officer. Good day," said Emily. The truck rumbled to life. She smashed it into gear. The scarlet-faced patrolman just managed to drag his motorcycle from her path. He started to pull his whistle from his pocket, then stopped. He pushed back his helmet.

"Aw, hell, what's the use?"

*   *   *

For the next hour Emily drove the truck around the city. Then, when she felt completely familiar with what she considered to be its eccentricities, she spoke again.

"Right. Let's go and collect the stuff from my place."

Emily's stuff was two heavy suitcases. They loaded them into the truck and drove to the museum.

"What are we going to do now?" asked Hettie.

"Put the suitcases in with the dinosaur, of course."

They parked the truck in the driveway of the Hayden Planetarium and lugged the suitcases round to the museum. Emily led the way to the dinosaur hall. She peered inside. The painters were working on the scaffolding at the far end.

"Watch where I go," she whispered. "Then follow me. Make sure no one sees you."

The Scots nanny watched as Emily, her suitcase under her arm, scurried towards the dinosaur. She lifted the edge of the canvas that covered it and burrowed her way underneath. Hettie followed a second later. They met in the darkness.

"Smells funny," said Hettie. "Like auld cemeteries."

"Imagination," whispered Emily.

"Really, like damp vaults."

"Hush woman. The only smells in here are from the dust and the canvas. Talk quietly or we'll be heard."

A painter was singing. His voice echoed round the square, almost windowless walls of the Early Dinosaur Hall. Emily pulled a torch from her pocket and shone it around the large tent made by the canvas.

"If I keep it low, it won't be seen."

The inside of the dinosaur tent brought back memories. It was a garden party marquee. Thunderclouds made it dark. It smelt of crushed grass and ale. The guests crowded together out of the rain. A sixteen-year-old Emily Biddle carried her first infant charge. In the twilight, a masculine hand slid over her rump and squeezed her bottom. She stamped down, hard, backwards. An hour later, when guests were being intoduced to the bishop, she was surprised to see the local vicar limping badly.

Emily jerked herself back to the present. The torchlight shone on the twelve foot high spine of the dinosaur that formed the ridge of the tent. The canvas draped down, and was supported, a few yards away, by two smaller dinosaurs, which held the tarpaulin walls on either side of the brontosaurus. There was plenty of room to walk around. Emily moved the two suitcases close against the foreleg of the monster.

Emily removed her pince-nez, polished them carefully with a paper tissue, and jammed them back on the end of her nose. She tilted her head backwards and probed the darkness of the canvas roof with her torchbeam.

"You were right, Hettie, my dear," she said at last. "It really won't make much difference to the shape of the tent if we DO take the bones off the frame." She tapped the metalwork supporting the fossilised skeleton. "Yes," she mused. "From the outside it'll look almost the same."

"Sa-a-nta Lucia," sang the painter. Even the dampening effect of the canvas between him and the nannies couldn't disguise his undisciplined voice. Hettie shuddered, and glanced at her watch.

"We really mustnae leave the bairns too long with Melissa and Susanne," she said. "Let's away back to them."

Emily parked her torch on one of the suitcases, and lifted the front edge of the canvas again. Then, on hands and knees, she peered out into the hall, like a rabbit emerging from its bolt-hole. The singing painter was standing on the scaffolding, his feet wide apart on the planks. He was clutching his stomach with one hand, while the other brandished a dripping paintbrush skywards. He was trying unsuccessfully to sing a high note. Emily shrugged the tarpaulin off her shoulders, and wriggled free. Hettie joined her in the corridor.

"Tonight," whispered Emily, confidentially, as they walked down the stairs to the entrance hall, "I shall come back with Melissa and we'll start work."

"Tonight you'll be in bed," corrected Hettie, firmly. "You've done more than enough, already. We caused the trouble. It's only right that we should be the first to take the risk."

"But, my dear girl, you can't work on your own," protested Emily. "I think a better plan would be for the two of us—as we're the oldest—to come in here together tonight.

We can help each other, and if anyone's going to get caught, it'll be us."

"You dinnae have to come," said Hettie, weakening.

"Pish . . . wouldn't miss this sort of a skylark for anything," giggled Emily. "I feel younger already. Fifty-five at the most."

"And what do we do about the bairns?"

"Melissa's free," replied Emily.

*　　*　　*

"They're at it again, Barthie," said the stout, elderly woman. She peered round the tubbed bay tree at the edge of her roofgarden and stared down at Randy and Melissa lying sun-bathing, two floors below on the neighbouring penthouse patio.

"Ah, gee," said Barthie. He buried the top of his tanned scalp even deeper into the comic section of his paper.

"They've got no shame, those two," said the fat woman. "He's kissing her."

"Sure."

"She's kissing him back. She's real loose. Oh, gee, Barthie . . ."

"Yeah?"

"He just undid her bra. He really did. Oh, lord, he just took her bra off."

"Sure, Freda."

"Oh, papa, you should see this. He's pushing her down on the sun-bed. He's kissing her again. Lord, he's kissing her boobs. She's biting him. Sure as God, she's biting him."

"Yes, Freda, hon." The paper rustled.

"Oh, goshakes. Now he . . . he's pulling down her pants. Right down. They're round her knees. Oh, God . . . he's looking at her. The hussy, she likes it. She just kicked the pants off. She's lying there. Oh, Jesus, Barthie, he's got his hands on her."

"Sure, Freda."

"Oh, my, Barthie. He's kissing her again. All over, this time. Her stomach. My gosh!"

"Yeah?"

"Now she's got her hands in his swim shorts. God, Barthie. She's got them off. She's scratched him. I can just see the marks on his back. Oh, God!"

"Sure . . . oh, God."

"She's got hold of him. That lousy little hooker! He's on her, now. Christ Almighty, they're doing it! Here, look . . . come here, look. Jesus, God, they're doing it. In public, too! Come up here, you lazy crumb. Come here and look."

Freda beckoned him, wildly. Barthie wheezed out of the canvas chair.

"The glasses . . . Jesus . . . look here through the glasses." She held the binoculars towards him.

"Freda, hon," said Barthie, wearily. "I guess it's time you and me went inside."

"You gonna manage, Barthie?"

Barthie pondered. "I guess maybe. But, hon, it's the second time this week." Barthie was sweating. He looked forward to the cold of winter, when people didn't sunbathe on rooftops.

Randy bent over and kissed Melissa's shoulder. Fluffy blonde hairs along her spine glinted in the sunlight.

"This is how I like to spend my mornings."

"But it's afternoon."

Randy looked at his watch. "And my afternoons, too."

A phone buzzed.

"Goddammit," moaned Randy. He reached out and selected a telephone from the collection on the iron table. "R.A.J. here . . ." He continued to caress Melissa with his free hand. "Oh," he handed her the telephone. "It's for you." He lowered his head again and kissed the gentle curve near her armpit. She wriggled.

"Hello, Melissa here. Oh, yes, Nanny Hettie. Yes, of course I will. No, he won't mind. Certainly. Around four. Goodbye."

72

Randy ran his tongue gently along the slim muscle that led him, almost by accident, to her breast. "You taste salty." He bit her.

"Ouch!" She slapped him. "You're a sadistic little boy." She grabbed his arm and bit back. Randy squirmed. "I have to go out and babysit this evening," she told him.

"Hell," he said. "I'll get frustrated."

"And I'm staying the night at Nanny Hettie's."

"Can't," said Randy.

"Can. It's my day off, remember. You'll have to put yourself to bed."

Randy sighed, then his face brightened. "You going to arrange a baby-sitter for ME? A cuddly 39-22-35 blonde will do fine."

Melissa bit him again. He caught her, and they wrestled on the sun-bed.

"Once more, before you go," he murmured. He slid his hand slowly from her shoulder to her breast, then down to her thigh. And glanced up, curiously, at the bay tree on the neighbouring rooftop.

*　　　*　　　*

Just before the museum closed for the night, Hettie and Emily walked in through the entrance hall again, and climbed the staircase to the dinosaur gallery. Hettie's stout figure was even grosser. She was pregnant with the sixty feet of rope she had wrapped round her waist.

"If it's like this, then we're glad we never had children ourself," she muttered.

"What's the matter?" asked Emily. She carried a large hatbox, heavy with tools and other pieces of equipment.

"It's that rope. It scratches, and it feels like it's shrunk, too. We cannae breathe." Her face was strained.

"Hold out a little longer, my dear," Emily encouraged. "We're nearly there. One more flight."

The dinosaur hall was deserted. The painters had left.

Emily looked quickly along the dusky corridor. There was no one in sight. She held a finger to her lips, then listened. It was quiet. She pointed towards the edge of the canvas sheet.

"Right. Let's get under it."

She burrowed her way into the dark interior. Hettie watched the canvas hump until the old nanny was obviously through, then she followed.

"My word, this really is romantic," said Emily, her nose twitching happily as Hettie crawled into the beam of her torch. "Sort of like being swallowed by the dinosaur."

She shone her light upwards. The stalactite ribs seemed to move in the wavering ray.

"We hope it's going to be safe in here," said Hettie, huskily. She gasped as the flashlight moved and rested on the beast's great head. She couldn't suppress a shudder.

"Stop it, girl. It's been dead for two hundred million years."

"We dinnae care about that," said Hettie. "Being dead two hundred million years only makes it more dead."

Emily swung the torch round the tent.

"Everything else is okay. Nobody's touched the suitcases. Help me unpack." The cases seemed to contain everything. Cooking equipment, rags, dusters, washing material, blankets, sleeping bags and inflatable mattresses.

Emily adjusted her wandering pince-nez and hung an electric lantern from the ribs of the dinosaur, and switched it on. "Nobody'll see this through the canvas," she said.

She unbuttoned her uniform. Hettie was surprised that her friend's underclothes were a pair of jeans, rolled up above the knees, and a tattered old sweater.

"You'd better change before you get your uniform dirty," Emily advised. "I put some overalls for you in that pack near the air-bed."

She took a screwdriver from the hatbox and examined the tail of the monster. "You use the wrench."

Hettie looked in the hatbox.

"What's a wrench?" she asked.

Emily moaned, came over and found it for her.

"You use it like this," she said. "You adjust it by turning this bit until it fits the nuts you want to undo. Now, let's hurry. We've got to get as much work done as possible tonight."

Hettie fiddled for a while. There was a loud clang.

"Shhh," Emily's voice was a stage-whisper. "What's the matter now?"

"We cannae undo any of the square things. It's impossible. They're all much too tight."

"Here, let me try." Emily expertly re-adjusted the wrench and fitted it on the nearest nut. It loosened. "There you are, no trouble."

"Oh." Hettie noticed that the nuts turned in an anti-clockwise direction.

Once she had mastered the technique, the job seemed fairly easy. Whenever one of the backbones was free, they lifted it down carefully and laid it to one side of the tent.

Emily worked quietly away, the perspiration mingling with the dust on her face. She looked like an eccentric professor at work in the burial chamber of a pyramid. The work became more difficult later, when they had to stretch to reach the ascending vertebrae. As the back arched higher, the bones became larger and heavier. Hettie consulted her watch. It was midnight.

"Let's try a leg. Then we'll call it a night," said Emily.

"You sound as though you're ordering an Aberdeen fried chicken, not dismembering a dinosaur," sighed Hettie. But, above her, Emily had already begun loosening the huge thighbone. She grunted. There was a creaking noise.

Hettie looked up quickly, in time to see her dangling from the top of the thighbone as it swayed away from the main structure.

The metal stay supporting it bent slowly, and gently deposited Emily back on the ground.

"Great grief, I thought I was about to become the first

person killed by a brontosaurus for two hundred million years," said Emily.

"Och, you will be if you try doing things on your own."

"That's enough, I suppose," said Emily. Her nose was twitching at a lower speed than usual. She was tired. "It's hard work filleting a dinosaur." She looked behind her at a neatly stacked heap of bones, then sat on one of the largest vertebrae. "We'll wash and then turn in."

The two nannies cleaned themselves as best they could with the damp sponges Emily had packed in the toilet hold-all. Then they snuggled down in their sleeping bags. A few minutes later they were asleep.

*　　*　　*

A clattering woke them. It was followed by an off-key rendering of 'Granada'. The painters were back in the hall.

"What's the time?"

Emily fumbled for her glasses and peered at her luminous pocket watch. There was no light beneath the canvas, even in daytime.

"Eight thirty."

"We've got to be away soon," hissed Hettie.

It took them twenty minutes to tidy up the interior of the tent. Then they washed themselves again, donned their uniforms, and slid out from under the canvas. The public entrances were still closed, so Emily led the way down to the staircase leading to the basement. She walked confidently towards the smell of food in what appeared to be the kitchen. There were several men inside. She poked her head round the corner just as a chef appeared.

"Have you got any jobs going?" she asked.

"Guess not, lady," he said. "Try later when the canteen manager gets here."

"How do we get out, then?"

"The way you came in," said the man.

"I'm lost. I can't remember."

76

The man pointed down the corridor.

The two friends made their way past the tinsmith's shop and the carpentry bay, to the shipping department. Emily paused. "Wait for me. Just a minute," she told Hettie. She looked around to make sure they were alone, then she reached through the service window of the office and snatched a handful of paper.

Hettie was horrified. "Emily Biddle, that's stealing."

"Borrowing," corrected Emily. "They're only sticky labels. I've got to have some for part of the plan."

Hettie pushed open the exit doors and the two nannies stood on the loading ramp, in the morning sunlight.

Emily blinked cheerfully. "I told you . . . it's going to be easy." Her face twitched and wrinkled as she grinned. Her pince-nez popped off the bridge of her nose. She twirled them on the end of their cord and started to sing.

"Rule-Britannia . . . Britannia rules the waves."

*   *   *

Lui Ho looked at the row of mildewing police uniforms hanging along the wall of the Tse Eih Aei sewer head-quarters. He hoped the nanny-ladies wouldn't take too long over the robbery. Not only did he consider the wearing of capitalist uniforms offensive to the People's Republic, but he regarded the hire fees of five dollars a day as extortionate.

"Line up," Lui Ho ordered his men, who were changing back into their loincloths.

"Reports, please," he demanded.

"We walked the beats, like New York policemen, just as you suggested, Comrade Leader. A most enlightening experience," Sam Ling announced.

"So?" demanded Lui Ho.

"We kept the people away from the museum exactly as planned." Sam Ling pulled out a notebook and began to read. "Nine forty-five—moved on young couple commit-ting sinful offence on public bench in front of museum main entrance. Nine fifty-one—found same young couple three benches farther along road . . . reminded them of obligation to state. Ten thirty-seven—dispersed small crowd gathered to watch behaviour of the young couple on grass of planetarium. Eleven thirty-eight—stopped car and issued severe warning on dangers of careless driving . . ."

Lui Ho held up his hand. "You did what?" he asked, incredulously.

"Issued severe warning," repeated Sam Ling. His moustache smiled at his boss. "A small joke of mine, Comrade Leader. The car was carrying the chief Soviet representative to an emergency meeting of the United Nations."

5

Fat Choy blinked the tears out of his eyes, and dabbed his handkerchief at the thin line of blood dribbling from his nose on to the front of his police uniform. He sat on the low wall of Central Park, opposite the museum entrance, until the waves of dizziness stopped and he could see properly again.

The five nannies had all arrived and were gathered, like a clutch of white hens, at the bottom of the museum steps.

"I've never theen that before," Susanne nudged Melissa, and giggled. She pointed at Fat Choy. "That policeman thitting over there on the wall. He must be very new. You know how nicely they all twiddle their night-thticks. Well, he can't. He just hit himself on the nose with his."

Hettie looked at her friends. "Everybody's here, then?

Nae too many problems, we hope, arranging for tonight off?" The nannies shook their heads. "Well, now, we think we begin by synchronising our watches, don't we, Emily?"

"Definitely," said the old nanny, her nose twitching faster with excitement. "Always synchronise watches before a big military operation. And, by the way, I think we should call this one by a code name, so we can maintain absolute secrecy. In future, we won't use the word dinosaur. It's to be referred to as Sassenach. It can even be our password, in the dark, in the museum. Everyone agree?"

Susanne squeezed Emily's arm for attention. "But pleath don't shoot if thomeone thays thathenach."

Hettie frowned.

"Ready with your watches, everybody?" she asked. She fidgeted while her friend, Emily, hoisted in half a yard of silver chain, like a battleship weighing anchor, to reach her massive silver timepiece. "We'll start counting," began Hettie. "Five . . . four . . . three . . ." Her voice cracked, and she sighed as she remembered the last count-down on the museum steps. "It's no use, we can't manage to count here."

Emily consulted her clock, dangling it on its chain. Her eyes followed it, as it swung like a pendulum, in front of her twitching nose. "At the third stroke," she said, briskly, "it will be four thirty-two, precisely . . . pip—pip—pip."

The nannies adjusted their watches.

"We'd better split up, now," advised Hettie, her voice strong again. "Action stations! In we go, in ones and twos. We'll meet on the fourth floor at four forty-five exactly. Tally ho, girls!"

The museum guard stood at the entrance to the Early Dinosaur Hall. "Och, dear," Hettie muttered to herself. "How on earth can we sneak in with him around?"

She stopped short of the doorway, and pretended to study a case of fossilised eggs. Then she checked the time on her watch.

"Make mine a three-minute one, Nurse," said a voice.

She turned. It was the guard. Hettie gazed at him, thoughtfully, wondering if she could find a quick way of luring him from his post. Suddenly, her problem was solved. A weird noise burst from the far end of the hall, and a strange, portly figure lurched into view, singing a wavering off-key Oriental melody, and hiccupping and belching alternately.

"Holy cow," grunted the guard. "A drunken gook."

He drew himself up, authoritatively, and strode down the corridor. The drunk disappeared round the corner. Hettie watched the guard follow him. There was a babble of confused argument. Gradually, it died away into the distance.

The other nannies joined Hettie.

"What was all that about?" asked Melissa.

"A drunken Chinaman," said Hettie. "Just as well he was there, otherwise we might have had trouble with the guard. Quick, let's get to work, now, while no one's around."

She led the way into the hall, and held the edge of the canvas covering the dinosaur, while the others crawled in underneath.

"It's ever tho exciting," whispered Susanne. "Like midnight feathts and pillow fights."

"Sush . . ." warned Emily, switching on the lantern she'd suspended from the skeleton the previous night. "Keep very quiet, and you'd better change into your working clothes." The old nanny was carrying a duffel bag by its string. She hung it near the lantern, on one of the bolts that had previously held a tail vertebrae.

"It's quaite dirty in here. As black as Newgate's knocker," remarked Una, wiping her finger along one of the bones. "We'll be quaite filthy by the morning."

"Hurrumph," snorted Hettie. "HONEST dirt's no sae bad. It comes off wi' a scrub. Plenty of hot water, soap and a scrubbing brush. That's what we taught the royal children . . . and a good hot bath EVERY Friday night . . . And look at them now."

Melissa smiled in the dim light. "I can see now why Miss

Emily says you were the power behind the behinds on the throne."

The museum was soon asleep, but inside the dinosaur tent the nannies worked away in the yellow light of the lamp.

The removal of the neck bones now meant a mountaineering attempt every time one was loosened.

"Got to get some steps," said Hettie. "Melissa and Susanne trot outside and borrow one of the painter's ladders."

The two young nannies sneaked out of the canvas tent, unlashed one of the ladders from the scaffolding, and dragged it back under the tarpaulin. It made the work a lot easier. Hettie climbed up to the shoulders of the brontosaurus and for two hours levered away with her wrench.

Eventually, she spoke. "You know, there IS something we forgot," she said, peevishly. "We must go."

"I'll come with you," said Una.

"All right," said Hettie. "Where is it?"

"Where'th what?" asked Susanne.

"The ladies', of course. What did you think we meant, the Braemar Gathering?"

"I'd like to come, too," said Melissa. "I saw one downstairs."

Emily lifted her duffel bag off the dinosaur frame. "Let's all go."

"Your washing things?" asked Una, looking at Emily's bag.

The old nanny shook her fuzzy head and poked her pince-nez back into place. "No," she said. "It's Tarzan."

"Tarzan?" Una looked horrified.

"It's who?" asked Hettie, startled.

"Tarzan," Emily repeated. "He fretted last night. Wouldn't sleep, pulled out nearly all his feathers. Today, he wouldn't eat. I couldn't leave him again, so I brought him."

"You must be a loony, woman, bringing your parrot along on a thing like this. Holy haggis, leave him up here, or he'll scream the place down."

"No, I shan't. I can't," said Emily, firmly. "If I leave him here on his own, he WILL scream the place down. He has to know I'm near. He'll be quite all right."

Hettie sighed. "Och, come on, then." She led the way out from under the canvas, and into the museum corridor. The building looked bigger by flashlight. Macabre shadows stirred among the trapped exhibits, as Hettie shone the beam from side to side.

"Round here." She back-tracked down the first staircase, followed by her platoon. "Shhhhh." Another light glimmered ahead of them. "It must be a guard," she whispered. They all pressed themselves against the wall. The light glowed for a few minutes, then disappeared. They heard the man cough in the distance.

"Surely there was a ladies' on the dinosaur floor," said Emily, clutching the duffel bag to her bosom.

"The only one I've noticed was on this floor," whispered Melissa. "It was near the elephants."

Just ahead of them, in the darkness, the herd of pachyderms lumbered and trudged, in frozen action, with their trunks bellowing soundlessly, and their eyes glinting blindly.

"Maybe it's somewhere here," breathed Susanne. "Use the torch again."

Hettie switched it on. Susanne jumped. "A man," she squeaked in a horrified voice. "A naked man. I thaw him. Disguthting."

"Shhh. It's only a model, lassie. We know the one. It's a Montana Indian, shooting birds. The toilet's away over there."

The guard's cough, close at hand, startled them. Una grabbed Hettie and pushed her into the plastic undergrowth of the Indian display. They crouched near the Indian. The others scattered.

Una glanced up at the figure, and felt her nose tingle. Don't be foolish, she told herself, it's a model, not a man. You can't be allergic to it! It didn't seem to matter. Her

82

nose still threatened to sneeze.

The cough sounded closer. A flashlight illuminated the display. Then the beam swung downwards as the guard hung the torch on a hook on the wall. The man leant back against a cabinet, fished a paper bag from his pocket, and took out a sandwich. He munched for several minutes. From another pocket he produced a hip-flask. He removed the stopper with his teeth, and gulped at the brandy.

"A noisy eater," whispered Hettie. "Bad upbringing."

"Shhh," hissed Una. She was suddenly embarrassed as she realised on what part of the Indian's anatomy she was resting her head. She blushed unseen in the darkness.

The guard swigged again at his brandy flask and started another sandwich.

"Och, he might be here for hours," murmured Hettie, her legs beginning to feel cramped. There was a slight scuttering sound behind her. "Shhhh," she said.

The leaves of the jungle display surrounding the Montana Indian rustled. In the reflected light of the guard's torch, Hettie and Una watched his jaw stop its champing. The man listened. The plastic leaves rattled again. To Una it seemed the guard was staring straight at her. He rested his sandwich and flask on the cabinet, and unclipped the flap of his gun holster. He pulled out the pistol and pointed it at the display. Una gulped. The guard then reached for his torch and swung the beam towards them.

Out of the foliage of the synthetic forest marched a strange, diminutive nightmare. Its ten-inch tall body was nude, apart from a neat crimson waistcoat around its middle.

"Oh, no! Tarzan." Una covered her face with her hands.

The small figure continued its swaggering march, like a clockwork barbecued chicken, straight at the muted guard. Hettie could see the beam of his torch quiver as his hand began to shake. Meanwhile, Tarzan goose-stepped on, until he was only three feet from the man. Then he unleashed his normal welcome.

"Ahhhhheee, ahhheeeee, aaaaaah . . ."

The ape-man scream echoed round the museum halls. The guard dropped his flashlight and pistol. The nannies heard his feet thudding across the polished floors. There was a crash as he collided with a display. Then a door slammed. The footsteps faded into the distance. Another door banged and there was silence.

"Och, my goodness," gasped Hettie. Susanne giggled. Emily chased after Tarzan on her hands and knees, and scooped him back into the duffel bag.

"Quick," said Hettie. "We've no much time. Into the toilet, and back upstairs again before we're invaded by the police. And for heaven's sake, Emily, keep a tight hold on that beastie."

Moments later, they were hurrying up the stairs towards the dinosaur hall.

"Phew," puffed Melissa, as they dashed along the last corridor, into the hall, and wriggled under the canvas.

Hettie watched Emily, as the old nanny adjusted Tarzan's bed inside the duffel bag. "Emily Biddle," she said, exasperatedly, "you're the sticky limit." Emily pretended she hadn't heard, and tickled Tarzan's head. "Hang that dratted thing up, and let's get on wi' the work."

"Oh, bother!" said Susanne.

"What's the matter, now?" demanded Hettie.

"It's all the excitement. I want to go to the loo, again."

"Goodness, child. Weren't you ever toilet trained?" asked Emily from the back of the tent.

"Quaite," said Una.

*   *   *

The dinosaur, beneath its canvas cover, was now unrecognisable. "It looks like a torture chamber," hissed Susanne, looking at the disarticulated skeleton. "Imagine thcreaming prisoners thwinging upside-down, dripping blood. And red-hot pincers." She stretched up and stuffed her fingers in the monster's mouth.

"Concentrate on what you're doing, child," gasped Emily, her nose twitching rapidly. She struggled to support the weight of the head as she straddled the framework.

"Take hold of it properly. If it drops, it'll swallow you." They lowered the skull to the ground.

Susanne nudged Melissa. "I wath thinking. I bet an expectant brontothaurus was really thomething."

"They laid eggs," Melissa told her. "They became extinct because whenever they climbed up to their nests, the trees collapsed."

"Poor thingth," said Susanne, sadly.

Emily slid down the iron support that had held a front leg. She rubbed the dust off her glasses and clipped them back on her nose. She surveyed the remains on the framework. "Not much more. Just the pelvis and odds and ends. I think it's time we all had a nice cup of tea."

An hour later, only the hip bone remained bolted to the brown tubing. Emily pulled up the baggy front of her overalls and wiped away a faceful of perspiration. The dust turned the sweat into a layer of mud. "I've got to make some sort of a pulley system to take the weight of that heavy piece. When we've got that down, we've almost finished."

*   *   *

Lui Ho trod carefully along the night-dimmed path, just inside Central Park, and parallel to the road running past the front of the museum. He held his nightstick, nervously, and kept reminding himself that his police uniform was probably good protection against being mugged.

Lui Ho wondered what Central Park bandits did to their victims. If they were anything like those in his home province, they cut throats. On the other hand, some bandits in the border districts specialised in a quick kick to the victim's knee-cap. Lui Ho clipped the nightstick to his belt, tucked his chin hard down against his chest, to guard his windpipe, then stooped and clasped a hand over each knee. He hoped there wasn't another bandit standing behind him.

"Pssst."

Lui Ho tried to look up towards the hiss. He found it difficult. "If anyone attacks us and if the conditions are favourable for battle, we will certainly act in self-defence to wipe him out resolutely, thoroughly, wholly and completely," he said, quoting Mao Tse-tung aloud in English.

The flat voice of Sam Ling came out of the darkness. "Had I been an enemy, I would have been terrified by that courageous threat, and I would already be fleeing for my life. As it is, I remained because I was so impressed by the important readings, I could not resist staying until you'd finished."

Lui Ho wished there was sufficient light to see his second-in-command's expression. "A true worker can always find comfort and advice in the words of our beloved Mao," he replied. "A pity that the rest of you have not learned more from them. Had you done so, we would not now be suffering from fifty per cent casualties. And we haven't had a battle yet." He sighed. "Fat Choy's broken his nose. You've got an ear cracked by frostbite—and in New York on a hot autumn day. And Pi Wun Tun has been arrested for being drunk and disorderly in the museum."

Sam Ling grinned in the darkness. "All in the cause of our country, Comrade Leader. And was not the acting of Pi Wun Tun quite superb? He helped the nanny-ladies with his subtlety."

"Subtlety?" snarled Lui Ho. "Pi Wun Tun has as much subtlety as a fart! I caught a smell of his breath as they dragged him past. He was as drunk as a warlord."

Sam Ling turned his rising chuckle into a muffled cough.

*   *   *

Emily jerked on the ropes. She seemed satisfied with her complicated pulley.

86

"Right," she said. "Susanne, up you climb. Unbolt the bone. The rest of us will take the weight and then lower it to the ground."

Susanne swarmed up the iron frame and began work.

"Take the strain," called Emily, softly. "Now, Susanne. Give it a push as soon as the last bolt is undone." The four nannies hauled against the rope.

There was a creaking sound. Nothing happened.

"Try again."

There was a grunt from Susanne. She stepped onto the hip-bone, wedged her shoulders against the ironwork and pushed with both arms.

Emily's pulley system had been calculated to support the weight of the dinosaur pelvis. The mathematics hadn't included the added poundage of Susanne. There was a sound of clothes tearing and a squeal from Susanne. The ropes groaned. There was a dull thump as the young nanny rode the pelvis, like a bucking bronco, to the ground. She examined herself. Apart from her gloves, she was naked. She looked around for her clothes. There was no sign of them, or of the other nannies.

"Oh, gosh!" she gasped. "Where'th everybody?"

There was a muffled yelp above her. She looked up. A bunch of legs and arms, sticking out from a web of rope, was tied to the side of the brontosaurus framework. Susanne's cotton overalls, now shredded, dangled overhead on one of the bolts.

"Get us down, idiot," came Melissa's strangled voice. "You launched us. Come and get us down. Quickly!"

Susanne struggled up the framework and began loosening the ropes round the nannies. Hettie's head and shoulders appeared. She looked at Susanne, her face purple dark in the lanternlight, her eyebrows raised. "Good grief, lassie. How dare you? How dare you?"

"Thorry, Nanny Hettie," stammered Susanne.

"Get dressed, this minute," ordered Hettie, tearing at the

ropes across her chest. "Get down at once and make yourself decent."

"That lassie," groaned Hettie to Emily. "If she's gi'en her head, she'll grow up to be a courtesan."

Susanne dropped to the ground. She reached up and unhooked her clothes. They were unwearable. She wrapped herself in one of the jute sacks, and then began untying the nannies again.

"Dinnae EVER do that again," stormed Hettie, as she finally lowered herself down the framework to the plinth. She rubbed the bruises on her chest where the ropes had caught her. "Dinnae EVER parade yourself naked in company again. Absolutely disgusting behaviour. Nakedness is for the privacy of the bathroom—and nowhere else."

"Yeth, Nanny Hettie," said Susanne, meekly.

The five nannies gathered round the big pelvis. Emily prodded it. It was undamaged. She tried to move it, but it scarcely rocked. "It's the biggest problem we've got," she said, peering at it closely through her pince-nez. "But I know how to get it out."

"You're optimistic," said Una.

"Organised," smiled the old nanny, wriggling her nose. "Gather yourselves for the great effort, ladies. The big offensive. Flex your muscles for the final assault. Shoulders to the wheel and noses to the grindstone. The relief of Mafeking."

"Emily, please keep to the point," Hettie interjected.

"Er ... yes," continued Emily, her face flushing. "We take the bones, one at a time, along the corridor to the window overlooking the planetarium. Then we lower them on to the planetarium roof. We carry them across the roof to the parapet, and lower them again, to the ground. I think that's right, isn't it, Hettie?"

"Of course," said Hettie. "Mafeking indeed!"

"But we'll be seen."

"Nonsense, Melissa," said Emily. "I've parked the lorry in the grounds of the planetarium. No one will look up at
88

the museum windows. In any case, there's a big tree in front of the planetarium and we'll be shielded while we lower the bones on the last stage." She stooped and tugged at a bone. "Heave ho," she said, gaily. Her knees buckled. "Well, nearly heave ho. Give me a lift, Una, and hold up the canvas." She staggered down the hall, balancing the bone, like a milkmaid's yoke, across her shoulders. The other nannies, similarly laden, pushed their way out of the tent, and grunted along behind her.

"I feel like a thafari porter," gasped Susanne, as she swung her first bone down to join the others by the window. "My dreth tickles." She watched as Emily ran her finger expertly round the casement.

"See," said the old nanny, triumphantly. "No burglar alarms." She undid the catch and pushed the window open. "It's too high to be reached from the ground. It's nearly impossible to break into, and they didn't think anyone would want to break out."

"We hadn't even thought of alarms," admitted Hettie. "But how do we get the bones down there? It must be all of fifteen feet to the roof. They'll break if we drop them."

"The ladder, of course. We'll get it," said Una. She disappeared along the corridor with Melissa, and returned with the ladder. They lowered the end on to the window ledge and slid it out until its feet rested on the planetarium roof.

"You climb down, please," Emily told Susanne. "We'll lower the bones on the rope. Stack them near the parapet, where they can't be seen from the road."

Susanne nodded.

*   *   *

Sam Ling nudged Lui Ho out of his doze. "Wake up. They're here," he whispered urgently. Lui Ho sprang to his feet, dragged his copy of the Quotations from Mao Tse-tung from his pocket, and waved it.

"Every Communist must grasp the truth," he shrieked. "Political power grows out of the barrel of a gun ..." A hand over his mouth cut him off before he could begin again.

"I am prepared to accept your political motivation, Comrade Leader," Sam Ling's patient tones whispered in his ear, "but your actions are likely to compromise our plans most severely. It is hardly wise to shout our glorious slogans for insurrection in the middle of New York City."

"Why did you wake—er, disturb me?"

"The nanny-ladies," said Sam Ling. "They are beginning to bring out the fake dragon bones on to the planetarium roof. I feel, as you may have suggested earlier, we should now collect Nicky Po and Chou-Tan and go to the intersections around the museum, and direct traffic away from the building."

"Quite so," agreed Lui Ho. "To work!" He made a practice traffic signal.

"Excellent, Comrade Leader," said Sam Ling, resignedly. "But, for halting American automobiles, try doing it like this ... Yes, our salute. But with the hand unclenched."

*   *   .*   .

The mound of bones under the dinosaur tent diminished as the pile on the roof grew. The rooftop looked like an early Christian catacomb. The heap near the parapet spread back towards the green copper dome of the planetarium.

"All right down there, Susanne?" Emily asked, softly.

"Yeth."

"We'll go back and hide for half an hour while the guards do their rounds. You stay here. Keep out of sight in the corner." Emily pointed towards the nearest sheltered wall. "Don't move around. Stay hidden. See you soon." She ducked her head inside, and the window closed.

Fifteen minutes later the nannies resumed their work. There were now only fourteen bones left. The leg bones, the head and the pelvis.

"Gosh, stewph." Una strained to move one of the heavy leg bones.

"Hang on, lassie." Hettie went to her aid. "If we put it on sacking, we can drag it along the floor—like a toboggan."

They rolled the bones on to the jute bags and pulled them to the window. Then, using the ladder as a slide, and holding the weight of the bones on the ropes, they lowered them to the planetarium roof. Soon, only the pelvis remained in the dinosaur hall. The nannies stood round it. "Right, give it all you've got, on the word," said Emily, when they'd rested. "Okay, girls, now. H-E-A-V-E." They levered the giant fossil on to the sacking.

"It'll never go through the window," puffed Una, her hair sticking to her forehead.

"But we cannae leave it," panted Hettie. "It might be the bit with the message in."

Emily settled herself on the pelvis, and smiled at her friends. "I think I've already worked out the solution to this little problem," she said. "But we're going to have to trust to luck a bit. What we've GOT to do now is to get this thing to the service lift."

Melissa stared at her in alarm. "I hope you're not going to suggest moving the elevator. We'll wake up the whole museum."

"Quaite," agreed Una.

"No," replied Emily, calmly. "But what I DO suggest is letting the museum people do it for us." She studied the puzzled looks of her companions. "All WE'VE got to do is to crate the pelvis and stow it in the lift. I'm betting we'll be able to collect it in the morning from the shipping department."

"Never," declared Una's disbelieving voice.

"For certain," said Emily. "I'll guarantee it. Come on. The guards won't be back here for some time, yet. We've got to do this now. It'll be too late otherwise. Melissa, go and collect Susanne. We need everyone's help."

She laced a rope around the great bone. Then, sled-fashion, they dragged the giant pelvis, on its carpet of sacking, along to the service lift. It took a long time, and they rested every few feet.

"I've got blisters," said Una. "These gloves haven't helped much."

"Maybe. But dinnae take them off—any of you. Finger-prints, remember," warned Hettie.

They slid open the steel doors of the lift and hauled the pelvis inside.

"We're on the home straight, now," gasped Emily. "All we've got to do is to wrap this thing in sacking and parcel it up, so it looks like an official consignment."

"Thank the Lord we don't have an imagination like yours," chuckled Hettie.

They packaged the pelvis. For the next half-hour, the five nannies stitched, cut, folded and padded. They pulled, twisted and sewed. Cross-legged beside the parcelled bone, Susanne, in her sacking shift, licked twine ends and threaded sailmaker's needles. Like a frontier wife in an Indian raid, she loaded and reloaded.

"It's a beautiful bit of work," commented Una, when all the loose ends had been tacked into place.

"Maybe a bit too good," said Hettie. "It doesnae look like men's work to me. Melissa, for a start, herringboned one of the edges."

"They'll never notice." Emily gave the bundle a pat. "They'll just curse someone for giving them a little extra work. Anyway, I'm counting on the audacity of the idea to pay off."

She felt in the hip pocket of her dungarees and pulled out the luggage labels she had taken the previous day from the shipping department. With a ball-point she wrote on them, then tied them on to the sacking.

"So *that's* what they were for!" exclaimed Hettie. "But they say, 'Smithsonian Institute—hold for collection'."

"Yes—because the Smithsonian Institute calls here regularly for stuff. If it was for anyone else, the shipping people might query it."

"Supposing the Smithsonian Institute calls here before we do?"

Emily shrugged. "That's a chance we have to take. It's really the only chance in the whole business. But there just isn't any other way."

They left the packaged bone in the centre of the lift.

"It's got to be as obvious as possible," Emily told them.

The nannies returned to the window, clambered out and scampered down the ladder to the planetarium roof. They squatted against the parapet and rested.

"I could do with a cigarette," said Melissa.

"Have one of mine—they're the thlim, wife-beater's kind." Susanne held out a pack. They were immediately confiscated by Hettie. "Oh, Hell!"

"Young ladies dinnae smoke in public places. Nor do they use such expressions."

"The museum's closed," protested Susanne.

"But we're here. And *we're* public."

Emily uncoiled the rope used to lower the bones to the roof and knotted a loop at the end. She poked her head over the low wall and watched the street for several minutes, then she dropped the noose over Susanne's shoulders and pushed it beneath her arms, checking the knot again. "We're going to lower you to the ground."

"Thank heaventh. I thought you were going to hang me."

"Good grief, child. Just hold on tightly until you get down, take off the rope and we'll pull it up again. Then the others can lower me."

With a gasp, Susanne swung out of sight. The nannies, straining on the roof, heard her feet scrabbling against the side of the building. Slowly, they paid out the rope until it slackened. Emily looked over the parapet.

"All right?"

"Yeth." The voice seemed very far away.

Seconds later, a puffed Emily joined her in the shadows behind the tree.

"Anyone around?" she whispered.

"No."

"Then I'll get the lorry."

Emily trotted over to the blue Chevvy. It sounded like a tank in the darkness. She backed it against the wall, stopped the motor and climbed out.

"Send down the bones," she called upwards.

"Bring out your dead," said Susanne.

"Shhhhh."

They loaded the brontosaurus into the truck, then covered it with sacking and most of their camping gear from the dinosaur tent. By the time they had finished stacking it neatly, the tyres looked squashed, the springs sagged, but Emily was confident there was enough room for the pelvis. She clambered back into the truck and drove it the few yards to the parking bay.

"It'll be safe there till the morning," she said, when she returned. "Hey, you up there." She called softly to the three nannies on the planetarium roof. "Haul us back."

From the planetarium roof they climbed into the museum and pulled the ladder in behind them. Then they locked the window.

"We'll just make it before the guard returns," whispered Una.

They returned the ladder to the scaffolding. Then they all stood back and examined the exterior of the dinosaur tent in the early dawn gloom. It resembled a distant mountain range.

"There you are," said Emily, in a hushed voice. "It's almost the same as when we started."

The others nodded, wearily.

Back inside, it seemed quite light in the glare of the lantern. They looked at each other. Their faces were streaked and grubby, their hands, in their gloves, felt gritty and rough.

94

·"It's done!" announced Una. "And everything went to plan. Let's have a celebration cup of tea."

"No. I've got something better suited to the occasion," said Emily. She reached over and pulled a suitcase towards her. She dug inside. "Here's how confident I was we'd succeed." She held up a bottle that glinted green in the light. "Champagne."

The cork popped and a splutter of foam sprayed a vague winebow in the beam of the lantern. Emily wiped her mouth with the back of her sleeve.

"Pass up the cups." She measured the champagne into the plastic containers. "Here's to Her Majesty the Queen, Great Britain, world peace—and us," she toasted. The others murmured tired agreement.

"I still don't see why we all have to stay here. Why can't we go now?" asked Melissa, thinking about Randy in his warm bed.

"We dinnae all HAVE to stay here," said Hettie. "But at least three of us should, to clear up. And so we might as well all stay. Och, it's only for a couple of hours."

* * *

Sam Ling stood in the centre of his intersection, directing traffic away from the museum building. So far, no one had queried his reasons, but if he were asked, he had rehearsed what he would say in his Peking University English: "To pursue your present course could incorporate you among the vehicular conglomeration of high density ahead."

In his less busy moments, Sam Ling tried to find fault with his plan for hijacking the dinosaur from the nanny-ladies. He couldn't. The plan seemed perfect. The bugging devices in the nanny-ladies' rooms, and attached to their telephones, had given him—despite their guarded conversations—everything he needed to know, except the location of the proposed hiding place for the bones. This didn't worry him. His team had only to follow them. And the nanny-ladies weren't going to make any fast getaway in their old truck. Sam Ling smirked.

At the intersection at the other end of the museum, Lui Ho groaned. He urgently wanted to urinate. He looked for a suitable place. The entrance to a basement apartment looked inviting. He'd only managed to get halfway to the steps when a taxi appeared. He ran back to the centre of the road and turned the vehicle down the side street. He made for the basement again. This time, he'd just reached the sidewalk when a stream of traffic headed by an articulated truck came into sight. With one hand in his pocket, clutching himself in an effort to subdue the increasing ache, he walked, with difficulty, back to the centre of the road junction.

"Heh, Frank," chuckled the truck driver to his mate, as they obeyed Lui Ho's weird signal. "You see that cop, signalling us with one hand. He had his legs crossed. Bet he's got a tight bladder."

Frank laughed.

The truck driver made a quick circuit of the block until he reached the tail of the traffic he'd led into the intersection. Lui Ho still stood there, in the same position, looking like a ballet dancer frozen in the middle of a two-footed pirouette.

The lorry driver chuckled again. He obeyed Lui Ho's signal for the second time. Then, as he passed him, he jerked the air-brakes into a hissing roar. His mate pressed down on the motorway klaxon. The shrieking blast screamed into Lui Ho's unsuspecting ear.

Inside the truck cab, the driver and his mate laughed.

Lui Ho stood, unmoving, with Oriental stoicism, until the truck was out of sight. Then he grimly raised one damp leg, and shook it.

*   *   *

The museum opened. Emily leaned over and nudged Hettie. "Pssst. Wake the others. We'll have to start cleaning up now. Tell them to work quietly. The painters are back."

Emily scrambled out of her sleeping bag, crept across the plinth and carefully lifted Tarzan's duffel bag nest off the empty dinosaur frame. She peeped inside, careful not to disturb the dozing bird. She knew how Tarzan liked to welcome each new dawn. She pulled an elastic band from her pocket. "Sorry, dear," she whispered, clipping it gently over Tarzan's beak. He looked at her, affronted and cross-eyed. "Not for long," she reassured him. He blinked, balefully.

"Just look at my face." Melissa was examining herself in a small mirror. "My make-up's going on like concrete."

"At leatht Mith Hettie lets you wear thome," said Susanne.

Emily shone her torch around for the last time. She could see no signs that might give them away. The plinth, apart from the little piles of nuts and bolts removed from the bones, was exactly as it had been before—minus its showpiece, of course.

When they heard the chatter of visitors, Hettie looked out. She watched a party of schoolchildren being led down the passage at the entrance to the hall. After they had passed, she crawled out of the canvas tunnel and studied the painters putting the finishing touches to the paintwork at the other end of the room. Then, on hands and knees, she scuttled over to the corridor. There, she stood, took off her once-white gloves and poked them into her bag. She loitered nonchalantly, and waited until the others joined her.

"Split up, now," she said. "Go out through the main entrance, one at a time. Dinnae hurry. Just stroll." She paused and scrutinised Susanne.

"Lassie, you didnae wash very well—your neck's filthy. No time now. Off you go. Meet you all by the lorry in ten minutes."

She left the museum by the tall doorway, overlooking the steps where the 25th Earl had died. For a moment, she stood at the top, and gazed at them, sadly. Poor wee Maister

Quincey, she thought.

"Cooeee," called a voice. Hettie looked down towards the road. Una stood, waving at her. Hettie hurried down.

"Look," said Una, her nose wrinkling as she stifled a sneeze. She pointed at a man picketing the front of the museum. He carried a large sign declaring—'Bring Back Prohibition'.

"I think I recognise him," she told Hettie. "The guard. You know, the one Tarzan frightened. But I suppose I could be quaite mistaken."

"Wheesht! Come away, lassie," grunted Hettie. But she had a second look, and she wasn't so sure Una was wrong. She led the way round to the planetarium car park, where the others were waiting. "My God," she exclaimed, looking at the wheels with their weight-flattened tyres. "All we need now is a puncture."

The nannies climbed into the lorry and squeezed themselves on top of the packed bones.

"Hurrah, hurrah," said Emily, triumphantly, and with a rumble, and a smash of the straining transmission, she drove them away towards the entrance to Central Park.

"What about the pelvis?" Hettie asked her.

"You and I will get it this afternoon," replied Emily.

"Is there room in here?"

"It'll just fit."

*   *   *

Considering it was autumn, the end of a particularly fine summer, the British nannies sitting in Central Park that afternoon looked pale. Una stretched. There was little contrast between her face and her neat white uniform.

"I'm quaite shattered, dearies," she yawned. "And quaite glad that it's nearly all over."

"Jutht the dinosaur pel ..." began Susanne. The words were cut short by Hettie putting her finger to her lips. "Oh, yeth. Thorry, I forgot."

98

"If you and Miss Emily want to go and get the, er, Sassenach thing, we'll look after the children," said Una.

"Do they need anything special?" asked Melissa.

"Give mine the 'Old Soldier' treatment if it squalls," said Hettie. "Sing 'Old Soldiers Never Die', and whop its behind in time to the music. Dinnae spoil it. And dinnae give it anything to eat." She looked at Susanne. "Especially ice-cream."

"Just treat mine like any baby," said Emily. "We'll be back as soon as we can."

They collected the truck from the parking lot near Emily's apartment, and drove it back to the museum. On the way, Emily stopped, reached under the dashboard and produced a brown paper bag.

"Disguise," she smiled at Hettie. "Dust coats. Put one on. And these."

"Why do we need all this rubbish?" asked Hettie, eyeing the black wig, and the over-large sun-glasses.

"YOU'RE going in to ask them for the package. And I'M driving the getaway vehicle. If something goes wrong, just rush out and jump in. I'll keep the engine running."

"Right," said Hettie, but she wasn't really assured.

They drove on to the museum. Emily backed the Chevvy, cautiously, down the sloping pathway to the loading ramp.

"Good luck," she told Hettie.

The stout Scots nanny straightened her blue nylon coat, pulled her stomach in and squared her shoulders. The fluffy black wig embarrassed her. She was glad she could hide behind the sun-glasses. Tightening her lips, she marched imperiously inside.

"My good man," she snapped at the gateman. "We believe you have a parcel for us. Smithsonian Institute."

"Got any credentials, lady?" asked the gateman.

"Credentials, dinnae be impertinent." She scowled at him. "Have you, or have you not, got our package?" Her broad Scots accent made him nervous.

"I, er," he stammered.

"Come along, come along. We dinnae have all day to waste."

"It's here," surrendered the man. He pointed to the pelvis in its sacking overcoat, resting by the entrance.

"Help us get it in the van, then," snarled Hettie. "Don't expect us to carry it ourselves, do you?"

"Er, no lady." The man poked his head through a hatch in an internal door. "Hey, Chuck, Wilbur. Give me a lift, will you? Got a heavy package."

With a great heaving and grunting, the final part of the dinosaur was loaded onto the sacks covering the bones in the back of the Chevrolet, and then driven out of the museum grounds.

*　　*　　*

Upstairs, in the Early Dinosaur Hall, the painting gang chief climbed down off the scaffolding and surveyed his men's work. He wiped his hands on a piece of rag, then reported to the museum director's office.

"You can have your hall back, boss. We've finished. Maybe you'd give the okay before we clean up?"

Together they made their way back to the hall. The director stood at the entrance and admired the work.

"Fine," he said. "Looks good. You can take off the sheets."

The gang chief waved to his men. They grabbed hold of one side of the canvas sheet and pulled it, folding up the surplus as it slid towards them over the tops of the exhibits.

The head of the small stegosaurus dinosaur became visible. The sheet dropped free and began to rise over the familiar hump of the brontosaurus in the middle of the plinth. The canvas fell to the ground, revealing the naked iron framework.

The gang chief's mouth opened.

"Fine paint job, Harry," said the director. "Makes the place look roomier." He swivelled around to get a fuller view of the blue-wash ceiling.

"Er ... boss ..." the gang chief began, glancing at the bare frame.

"Just dandy," interrupted the museum director. "Right, get the place tidied up." He turned and strolled thoughtfully back to his office.

He sat at his desk, drumming his fingers on the polished ammonite fossil he used as a paperweight. The drumming fingers grew slower, until finally they stopped. He stared at them. Then he buzzed his secretary. She stuck her head round the edge of his office door.

"Ring through to Palaeontology," he said. "Ask Bill if he's got the bront down for renovation ... I'm going back down to the hall. Come and tell me what he says."

The director paced, nervously, back to the Early Dinosaur Hall. The painters were carrying out their ladders. The director stood by the door and stared at the empty space in the centre of the plinth.

His secretary padded up to him. "They said they haven't got the brontosaurus for renovation, sir." Then she followed his gaze.

"Oh, gee ..." exclaimed the secretary.

"Precisely!" said the museum director.

6

Fat Choy sniffed gently through his blue and swollen nose, and pulled on the wide steering wheel. "When I was a boy," he said, "I used to ride as high as this on a farm bullock cart." He released the wheel with one hand and fingered his sore face. "Tell me, Comrade Leader, why does every other espionage group in America have their own fast car, except us?"

"Cunning planning of mine," replied Lui Ho. "A different type of vehicle for every tailing job. It is better for disguise."

Sam Ling looked up towards the roof of the driving cab. "Very original thinking on your part, Comrade Leader." For once, he was glad he had nothing to do with the idea. "To think of using an obsolete fire engine is devious to the extreme."

Lui Ho smiled. "This way we get priority on the roads. All give way to us." He sighed at the thought of his own genius. "Keep close to the nanny-ladies, Fat Choy," he ordered. "Unwittingly they are leading us to the secret hiding place they have prepared for the fake dragon. It will be a simple matter for us to appropriate it later."

Fat Choy grunted. The nannies' truck was several vehicles ahead, wedged in the lines of home-going traffic heading down East 59th Street and towards the Queensboro Bridge. Fat Choy ignored a red traffic light, forced two elderly nuns to scamper for sanctuary on a road island, and played chicken with other traffic in his anxiety to close in on his quarry. There was the sharp yowl of a police siren behind them.

Fat Choy glanced nervously into his rear-view mirror. "Comrade Leader, I do not question your superior knowledge when you say I have priority on the road. But I hasten to point out that there is a motorcycle policeman following us ... overtaking us."

The speedcop pulled alongside the window and signalled, frantically. They could hear his voice, high-pitched above the engine noise. "Follow me," he screamed. "Quick—it's this way. A bad one."

"A fire," groaned Fat Choy. "Just what we need. What do I do now, Comrade Leader?"

Lui Ho looked sideways at Sam Ling. His deputy's face was bland. "Pull out, oh leech-brain," Lui Ho sighed. "Pull out and follow him." He reached behind the seat and pulled out a fire chief's helmet.

*　　*　　*

"Down here, I thought," said Emily, pointing over the side of the bridge. "Down on Welfare Island, near the hospital. There are plenty of disused buildings around there. No one'll ever think of searching them. And we won't be given a second look if we go in our uniforms."

"Good thinking," complimented Hettie. "Oops, look out."

Emily swerved the truck as a fire engine, led by a siren-screeching speedcop, passed them. "We go down here," she said, as they reached the large elevator that lowers traffic down to the level of the island. She edged the vehicle off the busy highway and on to the platform. It clattered to life, and dropped slowly down through the steel girdering. It stopped at island level. The roadway split, the best surface turning towards the modern hospital blocks, the cracked path disappearing in the direction of the old, now unused buildings. Emily followed the old road.

There was a rough parking space near the tree-camouflaged derelict buildings. She stopped the truck in the shadows, and the nannies climbed down.

They explored the buildings. Those nearest the bridge showed signs of occasional occupation. It was also clear that hobos had slept there. The corridors were bare, and dust was thick everywhere. Cracked plaster gaped on the walls and paint leant away from the woodwork.

Hettie found a building which still had the main door closed. She pushed it. It gave a little. She kicked it open. Inside, it smelt of rotting lumber, damp, and the river. "Here," she called. "It's the ideal place."

*　　*　　*

The cop braked his motorcycle to a skidding halt in front

of the United Nations Building. A crowd blocked Roosevelt Drive, watching smoke billowing, in noxious spurts, from the window of a second floor office. The patrolman jerked his machine on to its stand and ran back to the fire engine as it rattled to a stop behind him.

"Okay, Chief, it's all yours," he yelled.

"Sit tight," hissed Lui Ho to his men. "With a small amount of discreet obstruction the whole corrupt edifice will be destroyed."

"Hey, come on," called the cop. "What's keeping ya?"

"We can't go in there, we're not members," replied Fat Choy, eyeing the smoking building.

Sam Ling punched him in the ribs. "That sort of stupid remark could get us all arrested," he snarled. He turned to Lui Ho. "Comrade Leader, much as I, too, would enjoy the destruction of the United Nations' headquarters, this is neither the time nor the manner." He looked towards the crowd. "And these people seem to be expecting us to do something—fast. I don't suppose you got any instructions with this fire-quencher when you hired it?"

Lui Ho scrutinised the spectators. Sam Ling was right. They were losing their patience. He shook his head. "No instructions. Has anyone seen New York firemen working?"

Pi Wun Tun leant over from the back seat. "I saw a fire ship working once, when some big liner came into New York Harbour. It just squirted streams of water up into the air, and everyone there cheered and clapped."

"The very answer!" exclaimed Fat Choy. "Perhaps we should entertain this audience by climbing on to the cab roof and pissing like an ornamental fountain."

Sam Ling snorted. "We'd better get out. At once," he said. "I suggest we unroll the hoses, for a start. Nicky Po, you'd better see if you can find some water, just in case our tank is empty."

They scrambled out. Nicky Po jammed his helmet on to his head and ran straight into the open door of the vehicle. He sat down, heavily stunned. Sam Ling hauled him back to his feet and tore off the hat. Nicky Po's crossed eyes blinked. Sam Ling reversed the headgear so that the long brim covered Nicky Po's neck, then he thumped it back on. "Toad's spawn," he shouted. "Hurry up and find that water." Nicky Po staggered away.

"Look busy," Sam Ling ordered the remaining spies. Pi Wun Tun rushed off and reappeared with an oxygen breathing mask. He tied it over his face and mumbled something. "What's wrong?" demanded Sam Ling.

"Can't breathe in it," puffed Pi Wun Tun. Sam Ling reached into the fire engine and dragged out a narrow pipe attached to a pressure-cylinder.

"Couple this on," he suggested hopefully. Pi Wun Tun stuffed the end of the pipe into the hose of the breathing mask, then nodded. Sam Ling opened the tap on the pressure-cylinder. There was a gurgling sound behind him. He turned back towards Pi Wun Tun. The glass face-piece slowly filled with fire extinguisher foam ... white bubbles streamed from the valves at the sides. Pi Wun Tun struggled and snatched off the mask, retching and spluttering like an asthmatic Oriental Santa Claus.

Fat Choy ignored his friend's plight and grabbed the two-inch diameter brass nozzle of a hose, coiled round a reel at the back of the fire engine.

He ran, for two hundred feet, drawing the hose in a straight line behind him.

"Good man," shouted Sam Ling. "That'll be enough. Now bring it back."

Fat Choy returned, panting, the sweep of hose following him like a tired snake. He stopped thirty feet short of the engine.

"Don't fart about," bellowed Sam Ling. "I said bring it here."

"I can't," protested Fat Choy. "It doesn't reach."

"Of course it reaches—it started here." Sam Ling hit himself on his forehead with the palm of his hand. Fat Choy tugged at the hose again. "Overgrown mealworm," roared

Sam Ling. "Go and unwind it from round that lamp-post. THEN bring it back."

Fat Choy rushed off again, following the route of the hose.

A stout figure, in overlarge fireman's boots, clumped in front of Sam Ling and saluted. Its helmet, also too large, rocked from side to side. "You know that round canvas thing rolled up in the back of the truck? It says on it that it's a jump sheet," said Chou-Tan, his hat nodding as he spoke. "I have unrolled it and laid it neatly on the ground below the smoking window."

"Splendid originality of thought," replied Sam Ling, his moustache smiling.

"Shall I now go and tell the occupants of the building to jump?"

"By all means tell them," said Sam Ling, glancing at the sheet laid on the concrete sidewalk. "But I doubt if you'll be able to persuade anyone."

Chou-Tan hurried away.

"I've got some," puffed a familiar voice. Sam Ling recognised Nicky Po's legs, buckled beneath the weight of a brimming drinking-water dispenser, complete with plastic cups. "There's plenty of it. Enough for everyone to fill their bladders."

"Put it down, lunatic," screamed Sam Ling. "Go and help Fat Choy with the hose." He turned to Lui Ho. "Perhaps, Comrade Leader, when our delinquent colleagues are ready, you will be so kind as to turn the switch marked 'pump' which I saw on the dashboard?" Lui Ho nodded.

A loud thud, and a jeer from the crowd, attracted Sam Ling's attention. He looked towards the building. Chou-Tan lay face-down on the jump sheet, in a disturbed cloud of dust. Sam Ling hurried over and prodded the still figure. It raised itself on its elbows and shook its head, vaguely.

"You tripped?" asked Sam Ling.

"No, I jumped," replied Chou-Tan, with a wan smile. "There was no one up on the second floor to persuade, and it seemed the quickest way down. I don't think much of it as a lifesaving idea, the padding's not thick enough."

"Chairman Mao protect me," groaned Sam Ling.

"We are prepared," called Fat Choy. He and Nicky Po held the nozzle between them and pointed it towards the smoking window. The watching crowd went silent with anticipation.

"Switch on," shouted Sam Ling. Fat Choy and Nicky Po braced themselves against the expected pressure of water. The pump engine started with a mechanical screech and a series of rattles. The hose, where it joined the engine, began to swell. Sam Ling watched the bulge begin to move along the pipe. "Stand by," he shouted. The swelling approached the nozzle of the pipe, then hesitated. The crowd murmured.

A rat poked its head out of the nozzle, its whiskers quivering. It looked right, then left, then sprang out and ran into the building. It was followed by a second rat, then a third, fourth and fifth.

The crowd roared.

"You guys having trouble?" asked a voice. Sam Ling turned. It was the speedcop. Sam Ling decided to take the initiative. He unbuttoned the holster holding his fireman's axe and passed the tool to the policeman.

"You go," he said, authoritatively. "Go break window."

"Who, me?" protested the cop.

"Yes," said Sam Ling. He pointed, carelessly. "That window." The policeman looked at him strangely, then shrugged and walked purposefully towards the building. "And when you've finished," Sam Ling called after him, "break all the others you can." He turned back to Lui Ho. "That'll keep him busy for a while."

Lui Ho stuck his head farther out of the driving cab. "I've found two more switches," he said. "One says in American, 'ladder up'. The other, 'ladder down'."

"Most excellent, Comrade Leader. Perhaps you should turn the fire engine to face the building, then try the 'up' switch," suggested Sam Ling, politely.

Lui Ho manœuvred the vehicle until the cab pointed towards the U.N. skyscraper. Sam Ling gave him the thumbs-up sign.

There was a whirring sound. The ladder on the roof of the engine extended itself at an angle of forty-five degrees.

"Marvellous, Comrade Leader," called Sam Ling. "Just a foot more and it will reach the window. Push again."

The machinery buzzed for a second time. The ladder jammed itself under the window ledge. The smile set on Sam Ling's face as the ladder continued to extend, pushing the fire engine backwards. "Comrade Lead ..." he began.

The vehicle rolled on, quickly gaining momentum. "The brakes," shouted Sam Ling wildly, as the reversing fire truck built up speed towards the parapet at the far side of the road..

"Comrade Leader," groaned Sam Ling. There was a minor explosion as seven tons of red fire engine smashed through the low wall. With a blank face, Sam Ling watched it teeter for a moment—and disappear over the edge. Then there was a splash and a huge tower of water rose into view as the vehicle hit the East River.

The spies, with the crowd at their heels, rushed across the roadway and stood, awed, in the gap left by the runaway engine. Below them, only the erect ladder protruded above the muddy waters. They watched as the half-drowned figure of Lui Ho rose, choking, to the surface, and climbed painfully up the ladder to the top rung, where it perched itself, shivering. The five members of the New York Branch of the Tse Eih Aei drew themselves to attention, facing him, and saluted.

*   *   *

The 20th Precinct Station House in West 68th Street is one of the oldest in the city. Four and a bit storeys high, it's a brownstone building, grubby and unexciting.

Inside, it's little better. It wasn't designed. It's grown into what it is—a home for hard-working policemen.

It has no cells, but it has an automat which supplies cigarettes, iced Coke, and candy bars. Next to the automat stands the boot-polishing machine which the policemen clubbed together to buy. And alongside that, the Kleenex tissue dispenser. Now they are the calmest, coolest, best-fed, most highly-polished cops in New York City—and they keep their noses clean.

The desk sergeant sits behind a wooden partition to the right of the entrance. He's kept busy answering calls from motorists reporting thefts from their parked vehicles. There is seldom a big crime in the 20th.

The desk sergeant was answering his telephone.

"20th Precinct. Yeah ... yeah ... you lost a brontosaurus? What's ... ? A sort of animal? That's a lot of help. Did it have a name on its collar? Well, I ain't seen it brought in here. Try the dog pound ... It's a REPTILE? Look, bud, we got enough work on our hands without looking for lizards. It's not ... ? Bud, kindly make up your mind. Is it dangerous? DEAD ... ? Well, what you want it back for? You're the museum. Okay, okay, you lost a reptile ... Stuffed? Not stuffed, just bones? HOW MANY?" He dropped the phone. It clattered on his desk. He retrieved it and wedged it between his ear and a roll of fat that swelled above his collar. "How many tons? You're kidding ... sixty-six feet long? We'll get a car down there right now ... Okay, two cars."

He hung up the telephone, scribbled on a pad, and turned to the policeman sitting next to him.

"I got some furlough due to me, ain't I?" he asked.

"Yeah, thinking of going hunting again?"

"Thinking of going anywhere—maybe huntin', maybe fishin'. I just got a funny sort of feeling that suddenly I want to go on vacation. I think I'll go see the boss." He stood up and wandered over to his Chief's office. He knocked, waited for the sound of the Inspector's voice, then entered. A few minutes later he returned.

"Chief says I can take my leave starting tomorrow. I told him I needed a break. Haven't had one since last year."

"How come you want one so urgently?"

"I just got a feeling that anywhere except this station house is going to be the best place for the next coupla weeks."

He wandered over to the Despatcher's desk. "Here, Mike, better get two cars along to the Natural History Museum. They say they've been robbed."

*   *   *

The two prowl cars sirened their way back down 68th and slid to a halt in front of the 20th Precinct Station House. The car doors slammed open and four policemen raced each other up the steps and through the narrow entrance. They collided outside the Chief's office.

"Hold it, boys," called the desk sergeant. "What's the rush."

"Tell you later, Sarge, gotta see the Chief," one of them answered. He didn't knock, he just pushed open the door. "Chief, the museum—they're going crazy down there. Say a gang heisted their dinosaur ..." The man paused for breath. "It's worth a million bucks ..."

The boss of the precinct, a tough Deputy Inspector, was a man with a sense of humour. He had to be, to be a successful New York cop.

"Slow down, slow down. Suppose you tell me from the front." He listened, carefully, while the men gave him the details.

"What time you boys get the orders to go along?" He looked at his watch, then grinned. "Cunning old sonofabitch ... shoulda known something was cooking when he asked for furlough."

"When who asked for what?"

"Nothing," said the Chief. "Okay, I'll pass it on to the detectives upstairs. I'll tell old Dick Tracy myself—like to see his face when he hears about this one." He looked at the calendar on the wall. "Durn it," he drawled. "Seem to have used up all my own leave."

He walked through the muster room and glanced at the notice board. He looked around, furtively. With his felt-tipped pen, he drew a moustache and spectacles on a wanted notice. Then he climbed the stairs to the detectives' division.

*　　　*　　　*

The Chief of Detectives inherited, briefly, the museum robbery—and the wrath of the City Fathers.

"You got a soft precinct," they blared at him. "Just automobile thefts, occasional muggings, routine jobs. No trouble ... and what happens? Suddenly everyone goes to sleep and you end up with the craziest robbery of the century. The mayor's running a temperature of 110. And wants action. NOW."

The mayor's temperature was infectious. The 20th Precinct, as the sergeant had predicted, became extremely uncomfortable. Detectives rushed everywhere. Most of them didn't need to rush, but they knew the penalty of being seen stationary when this sort of a panic was on.

Matters were made worse by the second phone call of that afternoon from City Hall.

"Okay," the official bellowed. "Cool it at your end. We're handing everything over to Hooligan's Mob."

When news of this spread through the Precinct Station House, the detectives moved faster than before. The mere mention of Hooligan's name gave the Chief Detective paranoia. The old sergeant suddenly wondered if he'd got enough money to manage a kodiak bear hunt in Alaska.

The local radio station scooped the story—tipped off by the pretzel salesman outside the museum. But the robbery made headline news in the evening papers. The museum offered a 10,000 dollar reward.

The robbery caught the imagination of the American public.

By late afternoon, the Museum of Natural History was having record attendances. New Yorkers who had never been to the museum to see the dinosaur queued in the hopes of seeing the spot where it HAD stood. By nightfall, palaeontology was the 'in' thing.

*   *   *

The New York office of the Federal Assignments Research Team is in a new skyscraper in the East Side. The building has no name, and little to distinguish it from any other, except that its thick glass doors are medicine-bottle green. Behind these, shielded from outside eyes, stand armed guards.

Upstairs, the Federal Assignments Research Team go about their work. Their duties generally hover between internal security and counter-espionage. Sometimes, they take over the protection of the more accident-prone of the visiting Heads of State. And, occasionally, they're called in to solve a major crime that has baffled the police. Boss of the New York branch is Jumbo Hooligan.

Outside his office building, there gathers every day a crowd of newspaper-vendors, ice-cream salesmen, shoeshine boys, loafing roadsweepers and Chinese laundrymen. From time to time they join the queue at the telephone kiosk to phone in their reports. These men are spies. Russian spies. Cuban spies. French spies. Arab spies. Chinese spies, and even American spies who spy on the other spies.

Jumbo Hooligan's bureau is no more important than its four sister offices in other cities. The foreign spies keep tabs on them all. And Hooligan makes a point of knowing his share of foreign spies, personally. So long as they are following him and his men, gleaning small scraps of spurious information—just enough to keep THEIR bosses happy—Hooligan is happy, too. It keeps the spies out of mischief. And it means he always knows where to find them. He'd be a worried man if they weren't around.

*   *   *

Hooligan put down his telephone. He lifted the metal wastebin from its nest beneath his desk and placed it tidily on the carpet by his side. He stepped back, took a short run and booted the container against the wall. It clanged and rebounded. He leapt on it savagely and stamped it flat.

In the outer office, his secretary typed on, unperturbed. Downstairs, in the street, the spies looked up, murmured, and prepared themselves for the inevitable next step—Jumbo Hooligan's harassed appearance outside.

They looked at their watches. It normally took forty-five seconds from the sound of the wastebin destruction to Hooligan's arrival at the door. Once again, the spies noted, he was punctual. His heavy, six-foot, four-inch frame burst through the plate-glass doors. His grey crew-cut bristled between its twin partings—the one on the left was the usual parting. He was proud of the one on the right, because it looked like a bullet furrow. In fact, it was a spectator injury, caused by the propeller of his son's model aircraft. It made him look like a Mohawk Brave.

The spies knew immediately that today's problem was serious, because Hooligan dispensed with the usual enquiries and pleasantries. He passed through them with a brief series of nods and a curt, "Hi, Fidel, Petrov, Carl, Pierre, Isaac, Ahmed." He ignored Pi Wun Tun.

A police car waiting at the kerbside whisked him towards Yorkville. The spies followed at handbook distance. Hooligan took the steps of the New York mayor's home three at a time, flashed his pass at the guard, and disappeared inside. The news-vendors, ice-cream salesmen, shoeshine boys, roadsweepers and laundrymen set up their new pitches on nearby Franklin D. Roosevelt Drive, and prepared for a long wait. They were good at waiting.

Hooligan stood in the hallway and showed his identification card again. The girl smiled and pressed the button of her intercom. "Mr. Hooligan's here. F.A.R.T." She smiled at him again, innocently. Hooligan glowered. He hated the abbreviation of his department's title.

"Send him in," said the intercom.

Inside the suite, overlooking the trees and the East River, were two men. Hooligan's chief sat at the head of a leather-covered desk, tapping his teeth with a pencil. Hooligan's keen ear picked out the dental strains of Dixie. The second man stood facing the window, his back to Hooligan. He turned round, dramatically. It was the mayor.

"Hi, Evelyn," he said.

Evelyn 'Jumbo' Hooligan blushed.

*　　*　　*

The scar on Hooligan's scalp pulsated like an agitated mealworm. His left foot was resting heavily on the new wastebin in his office. He frowned at the bewildered faces of his team.

"It's the mayor," he thundered. "He says he wants US to find the dinosaur. And fast . . . damn fast. He says the world's laughing at America. We're getting digs in every newscast. The President's been riding him. Boys, we're right in the track of the tornado. This ain't shoplifting. This one is one bastard we've gotta solve. And, as the mayor says, fast."

Jumbo Hooligan walked over to the sleek mahogany door, locked it, and dropped the key into his pocket. "So none of us leaves until we've thrashed our brains on why someone would WANT to pull a weird heist like this. Then we'll mosey along to the museum."

He shrugged his jacket casually off his shoulders and hung it on the rapier nose of a large, stuffed sailfish on his wall. Its conceited expression annoyed everyone. It seemed to know that it was only two pounds short of the American record.

Jumbo reached for his shoulder holster. There was a nervous, automatic reaction from the tuned reflexes of his team. They relaxed as he drew a sinister-looking seven-inch aluminium tube from the spring clip. He unscrewed the cap and shook out the splintered half of a cigar. The men knew better than to interrupt him during this performance. It was Jumbo Hooligan's thinking space. He groped in his hip pocket and produced a stubby corncob pipe. He stuffed the cigar end firmly into the bowl, and snapped it off level with the rim. The remainder he put back in the canister, and the canister back in his shoulder holster.

He wedged the pipe between his teeth. He didn't light it. Hooligan was a non-smoker.

"So ... The President, the mayor, and me, we want that dinosaur."

"Sure, Chief, instantly," said Willie Halfinch.

Jumbo gave him the nothing look that he reserved for stupid remarks. The new boy's six-foot-ten-inch body squirmed. Willie was finding the height that gave him his All-American basketball stardom an embarrassment.

Jumbo Hooligan thumbed the switch of his intercom. "We're in conference," he snapped. "No telephone calls, no messages. Knock with a fresh pot of coffee every hour. And sandwiches. And, Sheba, make mine hot pastrami and cucumber, on pumpernickel."

"I gotta idea, Chief."

"What is it, Halfinch?"

"Shouldn't we get some hotdogs, too?"

*　　*　　*

The robbery was a lulu of a problem.

"It has to be the Cubans," mumbled Boots McGraw.

"But bronts don't fly," said Willie Halfinch. "If it'd been a pterodactyl, it would most certainly be in Cuba. They've hijacked just about everything else."

"Okay, cut the humour," glowered Jumbo Hooligan.

"Say, boss," said Huw Schwartz. "Maybe one of the local small-time gangs stole it."

"For what? They could have rolled a bank for the time and trouble they put in knocking off a dinosaur. And for what? Where d'you fence a fossil? What do you do with it?

Cut it into cubes and sell it to tourists? Nope ..." Jumbo poked his ear with his pipe stem.

"I've heard of art collectors who buy stolen paintings, just so's they can look at them. Keep 'em in a safe for years and only take them out for a gloat when they're alone. Maybe the dinosaur?" said Ivor Schwartz, hopefully.

"So what sort of safe do you keep that many tons of bones in? Would you like to haul 'em out every night just to take a looksee? Nope, whoever heisted this lot had another reason. They can't sell them. And they don't mean anything unless they're assembled to look like a dinosaur. I'm thinking of maybe ransom." Jumbo leant his backside against the desk and looked up at the ceiling. "More ideas?"

*　　*　　*

The third coffee jug was empty. Ulysses Pilgrim picked it up and walked over to the door, opened it and strolled out, and returned a moment later with a copy of the *New York Daily News*. He closed the door behind him and went back to his seat.

Willie Halfinch reached over and tried the door. He'd watched Jumbo lock it again after each fresh delivery of coffee. It was still locked.

"Hey! How d'you do that?" he asked Pilgrim.

The long-haired, hippy Ulysses looked at him.

"Do what, man?"

"It's still locked. The door," said Willie.

"Oh ... is it?"

"Go easy on Houdini, Willie," said Jumbo Hooligan's black deputy, Adam Gallows. "It's taken us eight years to train the guy. He's forgotten keys exist. There ain't a lock in the world he can't open."

It was a further ten minutes before anyone spoke. It was Willie Halfinch again. "How about the glue factory?"

"Willie," said Jumbo, patiently, "these are fossils, not bones. I'm going to tell you one thing." Jumbo's tone became
116

quiet and menacing. "If you open your mouth just one more time with some stupid suggestion, I'll have you taxidermified and stood outside my door with a handful of cigars for visitors."

"Students are a good bet. They've usually got a protest of some sort lined up," volunteered Huw Schwartz. He hiccupped, then belched loudly.

"I wish you'd lay off the chillis," said Huw to his twin brother, Ivor.

"Oh, Jesus," said Ivor. "I forgot."

"I always get your goddammed indigestion. You ought to be more considerate."

Ivor blushed.

Being identical twins had advantages in their work. But there were also drawbacks. The Schwartz twins' emotions stabbed between them like radio waves. They experienced each other's feelings, regardless of distance.

"I'm waiting ..." said Jumbo.

"For what, boss?" asked Huw.

"You've done everything else, I'm waiting for you to break wind."

"Sorry, boss ... chilli pickle."

"I'll check out the students," said Ulysses. "But don't expect a lead from them. They're my scene, and I haven't heard a murmur."

"I think we're wasting our time here," said Jumbo Hooligan. "We're overlooking the obvious. We're all looking for a big motive. I think we've got a nut, or a couple of nuts, or maybe half a dozen nuts. Let's not be panicked into illogical conclusions. The only way we're going to get the answer to this is by nosing around. Grab your hats, boys. We're going to the museum."

7

Jumbo Hooligan liked to picture himself as Master of Foxhounds when he and his team worked together. He stood now, legs straddled, looking into the twilight of the Early Dinosaur Hall, his pack assembled behind him.

A museum official eyed Hooligan nervously. He stifled a brief, imaginary picture of a stuffed Hooligan, on a small wooden plinth alongside the gorilla in the Hall of African Mammals. The men with Hooligan looked ugly—either hoods themselves, or yippies who would carve their initials on all the museum's most valuable exhibits. He decided to put an extra guard on the elephant display.

He particularly resented Willie Halfinch—because he was so tall. Tall men were invariably graffiti addicts, and they wrote their coarse poetry so high on walls it was difficult for him to read. Perhaps this human sunflower had been responsible for the slogans that had begun all the trouble.

He looked at the two men who were obviously twins. Short and black-eyed, they showed some sort of Mediterranean ancestry—and, as a blond, Nordic type himself, he hated short, dark, Mediterranean people.

He didn't trust the other members of the team, either. The black-skinned Adam was too quiet, and hadn't said a word since their introduction. He didn't like the hippy in overalls. And the other man, Boots McGraw, was clearly an Irishman. He couldn't stand Irishmen.

"Please take care of the exhibits," he said, nervously.

"We'd better. You obviously can't." Jumbo Hooligan

tossed the next sentence over his shoulder. "Right. Not a man in there until Pilgrim's given it the sniff." He turned back to the museum official. "You kept the public out?"

"We didn't let them in the hall. They just filed past the door."

Jumbo Hooligan glowered. "I suppose everyone on your staff's had a good scout around here?"

The man was eager to appear helpful. "Yes, of course. We had a very careful look round."

"Screw me," exploded Jumbo. "Why does everyone think he's a private eye? Okay, so you've made life a little harder for us." He glanced at the woodwork by the door. "You got a guard about five-foot eleven? Longish hair, sleeked back with hair-oil?"

"Well, yes. You know him?"

"No," glowered Jumbo. "Sack him. He's lazy. Lounges around too much."

"Yuh ... well, yes ... maybe," stammered the official.

"We don't want to be disturbed," said Jumbo. "Don't let anyone near here. Okay?"

The official decided to leave. He nearly escaped.

"Hey," Jumbo called down the corridor after him. "Your restaurant ..."

"What about it?"

"Tell them to send up a dozen hot salt beef sandwiches. Okay?"

"They're closed," replied the official. For once, he actually enjoyed lying.

"Not till four thirty," said Jumbo, calmly. "Tell 'em, on rye, with cucumber pickle." He turned away. "Okay, boys, set up the grid."

It took the team ten minutes to lay down a neatly measured grid of white ribbon throughout the hall. The tapes were pinned to the floor at the sides and ends of the room. The squares were then counted and numbered on a graph-paper pad that Adam Gallows carried.

Jumbo Hooligan looked at Ulysses Pilgrim and nodded.

"Right, baby, smell it out," he said.

Ulysses had been leaning casually against the corridor wall while the others worked. His long hippy hairstyle seemed out of character with his grey working overalls with their padded knees. The cuffs, ankles and neckpiece were close-fitting and elasticated, like a racing motorist's fireproof suit. A small leather pouch, containing his locksmith's tools, was fastened to his belt. He reached into a hip pocket and pulled out a pair of thin black gloves. He worked them carefully on to his hands, pushing the skin-tight leather firmly down his fingers.

He loped to the doorway, glanced around the long hall, then squatted for a moment on his haunches. He lowered himself on to his hands and knees, and, with complete lack of selfconsciousness, began an unhurried scrutiny of the hall floor—with his nose. Working across the width of the hall, then along its length, he sniffed, paused, made notes on a pad, and sniffed again. His complicated system search took him over an hour. At last he stood up—his face dusty, the tip of his nose black where it had occasionally brushed the ground during a close sniff.

"Okay, Jumbo," he called back. "I got it all."

"Say, Ulysses," Willie Halfinch looked curious. "What d'yer smell?"

"Dead brontosaurus."

"Gee!"

Jumbo Hooligan moved his great bulk into the hall. "File your report. Ivor, you check the iron framework."

He turned to face the remainder of his team. "Right. Now get busy. I want this job over. And, remember, fast."

There wasn't an investigation team in the whole of New York State to rival Jumbo Hooligan's. What made them unique was how they worked.

At this early stage they worked to an orderly and practised routine. Immediately Ulysses had finished, Boots McGraw worked over the same areas with a battery-powered suction-cleaner.

As he completed each square yard of the grid, he removed a plastic bag from the cleaner and put it into an envelope and marked it with a number. When he'd finished, he packed the envelopes into his executive case and left.

Behind him came Huw Schwartz, the squad's camera specialist. He photographed, in detail, every aspect of the hall, the plinth, the two remaining dinosaurs—and, because he was exceptionally enthusiastic, even Jumbo Hooligan and his fellow-members of the team.

Ivor, his brother, was the fingerprint man. He moved around with Huw, dusting, examining, and demanding even closer close-ups.

Adam Gallows, Hooligan's deputy, helped where help was needed. At this stage, he had little to do. His work would come later.

Willie Halfinch was the weights and measures expert, a sort of mobile mathematical calculator. Willie roamed around the hall, measuring, rechecking, and measuring again, just to make sure. He judged lengths, heights and distances relating to everything. He loved measurements. He was finding it hard to resist Hooligan's big feet. He guessed them at fourteen and a halves. Within an hour he had a list of measurements of everything on the fourth floor of the museum—walls, ceilings, corridors, doors, floor tiles, lift entrances, showcases, reconstructed skeletons and, for purely personal reasons, mental records of a rather pretty brunette schoolteacher escorting a group of pupils.

When he had finished measuring, he started weighing.

He hopped a lift to the basement, where one of the staff gave him a photograph of the missing exhibit and showed him to the Dinosaur Spare Parts Department. Here, long rows of shelves held various bits of fossilised brontosauruses —tons of them.

Willie removed his wristwatch—it upset his delicate balance. Then he picked up various bones and weighed them in his hands. He prided himself on never being more than a quarter of an ounce per pound out in his judgment.

After he had tried weighing a few of the smaller fossilised bones, he was able to estimate the heaviness of the larger pieces—without even lifting them. He studied a hefty pelvis lying on the floor, then jotted down its weight in his notebook.

Upstairs, on the fourth floor, the Dinosaur Hall was now almost empty. Only Adam Gallows remained. He stood in one corner, arms folded, just looking. Then, he walked around the hall a few times, stopping occasionally. He went into the corridor. He looked in both directions and then strolled down to the tall window. He examined the window frame, grunted to himself and opened it.

He made his way down to the ground floor and round to the front of the Planetarium. He liked to have a quiet and undisturbed look, on his own. By the time he'd returned to the museum entrance, a car was waiting to take him back to Hooligan's office.

Petrov and Carl, Isaac and Ahmed, delegated to watch Gallows, ran to their various forms of transport as he drove away. They had a lot to report, too.

*　　*　　*

"Sam Ling ..." raged Lui Ho, pacing around the small square of the sewer headquarters. "Has it occurred to you that many of my ideas, of which you constantly keep reminding me, may have been discarded by me BECAUSE they were NOT suitable?" He groaned. "Every genius has a weakness —even I. You exploit my weakness. My genius provides me with many wonderful ideas. My regrettable memory allows them to be forgotten." He swung round to face his deputy. "However, I do remember suggesting that we should totally destroy the museum, the fake dragon AND the nanny-ladies. Had we followed that suggestion, we would not be in difficulties now."

Sam Ling tried to console him. "That unfortunate fire

could not have been foreseen, even by your genius, Comrade Leader. It was responsible for our losing the prize we have sought so diligently. However, it will be a simple matter for us to redeem the situation by keeping a careful watch on the nanny-ladies at their residences. Sooner or later, they will go again to the dragon, and when they do, we will be there also." He smiled at Lui Ho. "If you so desire, when we have captured the fake bones, we can dispose of the nanny-ladies in any manner you think fit."

"The spin-drier," said Pi Wun Tun.

"After they have satisfied our personal pleasures," added Fat Choy, with slow emphasis.

Chou-Tan waved his two sling-supported arms, like a white bat. "I believe we have all behaved with true professional initiative at the fire. I feel we should be recommended for a People's Republic citation. We are indeed extremely fortunate to have such an inspired leader as Lui Ho, whose strategy in deliberately wrecking the fire engine saved us from the idealogical error of extinguishing a blaze in the United Nations' Building."

"For as little as a third of our annual espionage budget," muttered Sam Ling, under his breath.

"At times like these, I wish I wasn't an atheist," grunted Pi Wun Tun. "At least the Americans have got someone to blame when things go wrong. But we ..."

"Things do not go wrong for the loyal in the People's China," shouted Lui Ho. "I have not committed a single error."

"Only multiple ones," breathed Sam Ling, quietly.

"We will work according to the rules laid down in the People's Spy Manual by our beloved Chairman," continued Lui Ho. "We know the fake dragon is somewhere near the river, perhaps in chests on the river bottom. Even so, we will discover its whereabouts. We will follow the nanny-ladies at all times. You will stay closer to them than worms in a Mandarin's bowels. They will do nothing ... pick their noses, spit, pluck their armpits, scratch their arses, pass water, or clean out their ears without your knowing."

"I shall also make a note of anything to do with the fake dragon," said Fat Choy, conscientiously.

"Such dedication will ensure you long life," snapped Sam Ling. He turned to Chou-Tan. "Transmit to Peking that we want a submarine to stand off the coast, ready for the moment we need it. The rest of you—get working on those women."

*   *   *

Jumbo Hooligan pulled back the curtain separating his office from the operations room. He walked over to the long blackboard that was already marked into squares. He picked up a piece of chalk, counted squares on the board, and drew in the dinosaur plinth, and the wall cabinets of the burgled hall.

"Okay," he rasped. "Let's have it. What did you get, Pilgrim?"

Ulysses shook his long hair. He was back in his normal, eccentric clothes. He drawled. "I got ... er ... Boss, I got plenty. First, I got dust smell bad. Too much dust. Always get it in public halls. I got Central Park earth smell. I'd expected that, anyway, as the museum's next to the Park. I got plenty of paint smells, turpentine—you know, that sort of thing. And I got brake fluid smell near where the painters were working—maybe one of them stood in a garage on the way in one morning. I got the usual dog smells. I got good smells on the limestone plinth, though."

Jumbo Hooligan began chalking up a long list of smells on the board as Pilgrim continued: "The strongest smells were in the area D four to ten. I got good ones there. You're going to think I'm nuts, but I'm right. I got women smells. Not men. I got the smells of two, maybe three different types of feminine soap. And lavender. Very strong. I got a tea smell on square E seven. Leaves smell, not tea bags— with milk, not lemon. I got a deodorant smell on square D

124

nine. And I got a definite rubberised canvas smell in two separate places, covering square D four and E four and again at D eight and E eight. I also got a cheese smell and a bread smell on square C seven. One other thing I think's important. I got a talcum powder smell, very odd, on D one, two and three. I guess that this is where they crawled in under the canvas. The smell was very distinctive."

"Talcum powder and lavender?" queried Jumbo. Ulysses nodded. "Anything else?"

Ulysses checked his notebook. "Nope."

Jumbo swung his attention to Boots McGraw.

"I got quite a lot that backs up Uly's sniffer." He opened his notes. "My machine got the talcum on D one, two and three, the same as Uly. But I also got it in single grains in the whole of the area covered by C, D and E, six, seven, eight and nine. I guess the traces would be too slight for his smeller. It's baby powder. I got two small tea leaves in E seven. I had them checked out. It's a strange brand that Limey's drink a lot. Called Earl Grey—it's a perfumed tea. It's imported by Leo Mathieson's. Only sold in about fifteen shops in New York. I got a list of them.

"I got quite a few hairs—a mixture of male and female. Some of it'd been around for quite a while. Some was dropped recently. I don't think they're a lot of help at the moment, but they'll be useful when we have suspects to check out later.

"I got skin scales in several places, but mostly again in the D one, two and three areas. It confirms that this is where they crawled under the canvas. I also got two different types of stocking threads. One, on D two, is a coarse fibre, not used much today. I'd say probably the type worn by an older woman, or one with varicose veins. The second thread is from a cheap quality nylon—called Heaven's Above. These tights retail for about half a buck in most stores.

"I got the usual mixture of dust that you'd expect in a public place, but I got a crumb of bread in C seven. It was from a pre-sliced loaf, white, American flour. Could be one of several bakers.

"There were some various coloured wool fibres. A couple in very pale pastel shades. Some could have blown on to the plinth, or even have been dropped off the canvas sheet. Maybe useful; maybe not. Also got a couple of shreds of denim, from the framework. I'm checking that out."

He stopped for a moment, wiped his forehead with the back of his hand and continued.

"One good one. I found a flake of plastic from the top surface of a shoe. It's black. The shoes are imported but are produced specially in France for Denny Lewisham's Shoe Parlour des Dames on Lexington. He's only had three sizes in the range. They're straight fours, fives, and sixes. B fittings. Square toes. Low heels. Teenagers like them. That's about it."

"Good," said Jumbo Hooligan. He pointed at Ivor.

"I checked the plinth, Boss. Very difficult to find anything on the rough limestone. First, I went all over the two small dinosaurs. Plenty of fingerprints on those, but when I classified them, I found they could mostly be accounted for by the museum staff. There were a lot of prints on the bones nearest the guard rail, probably museum visitors who just stretched out and touched them.

"Then I checked the iron frame of the brontosaurus. Whoever worked on the frame wore gloves. I picked up some patterning in the dust on the frame, fancy stitching."

Ivor began to grin. "You want me to prove I'm going nuts, boss?" He paused. "I also got a nipple print near the top of the metal frame."

Jumbo stared.

"Sure boss. A nipple—you know, the strawberry on the sundae."

Hooligan's team laughed.

"Huw's got pictures of everything," continued Ivor. "And I had him blow up some of the bolt heads that held the bones to the frame. They're mighty interesting. Most of the hexagons are badly damaged. Whoever loosened them used an adjustable wrench. It was poor quality and sprung a little when they strained on it. Another thing, quite a few of the heads showed that someone had tried to tighten them before realising they loosened the other way."

Ivor interrupted himself.

"Mind if I smoke, boss?"

"Go ahead."

Ivor strolled over to Jumbo's desk. He flicked the lid of the executive cigarette box reserved for favourite visitors, and took out a Dunhill. Jumbo Hooligan started to speak, then changed his mind. Ivor lit the cigarette.

"I found some rope burns on the metalwork above where the big pelvis was. They must have jury-rigged some kind of sling to lower this bone to the plinth. I got some rope fibre. The lab boys say it's an artificial fibre—terylene. Judging by the width of the burns, the rope's the sort used by sportsmen, climbers or maybe yachtsmen. It's sold in almost all the sports dealers, but we'll check them out for recent sales. They don't sell much rope at this time of the year.

"That's about everything I got in the hall," he ended.

Jumbo nodded again. "You," he said, looking at Willie Halfinch.

Willie blushed. He was tempted to tell the boss his hat size, but he guessed that Jumbo already knew.

"The Hall's 136 feet three and a quarter inches long, by fifty-six feet two inches wide. It has 690 flooring blocks. Each block thirty-seven and a half inches long, by thirty-six inches wide. The stone plinth covers 155 blocks. The doorway is ten feet wide and ten foot tall. The wall thickness at the doorway is five and a half feet ..."

"Okay, okay," interrupted Jumbo. "Give me something I can use."

"Er ..." Willie blushed again. "Er ..." He looked up brightly. "Your feet are size fourteen and a half," he said.

"My what?"

"Er ... the limestone plinth weighs nineteen tons."

"Fine," said Jumbo Hooligan, patiently. "That'll be useful to know if they ever come back and steal that, too."

"A live brontosaurus, the same size as the one stolen, would have weighed just over thirty tons and would have eaten nine hundredweight of food every day."

"Marvellous," groaned Jumbo. "Now I won't have one as a pet."

"Oh! The weight of the skeleton was three and three quarter tons. I got some good stuff about the bones, though."

"You know how much soup they'd make?"

"Sorry, Chief. You want I should work it out?"

"Forget it."

"The bones range in weight, from the little ones of two pounds each, to the biggest, the pelvis, which I calculate at five hundred and twenty-eight pounds and seven ounces. It would take three strong men to lift it. They couldn't carry it far. Skid marks on the floor show it was dragged on some sort of thick cloth. Huw's got a photo record. The scratches go straight to the service lift and end inside. I couldn't trace them any further.

"The marks show it was dragged in very short bursts. I'd say that several people pulled it, not always heaving in the same direction. That's what bugs me. I'd guess ..."

Jumbo Hooligan stopped him. "You know the rules, Willie. No guessing at this stage. Only facts."

"I went on the planetarium roof. Marks show the bones were left there for a while. The heavier ones sank into the bitumen a little.

"I also checked the front of the planetarium and the car park. One of the leg bones left an imprint in the soil by the planetarium flagstaff. They only made one journey to take them away. They used a truck. I got a cast of the tyre tread. The truck would have to be at least a five-tonner. I got a lot of other measurements if you wa ..."

"Okay, okay," barked Jumbo Hooligan. "We know you got them if we need them."

He stepped back and looked at the now long list of items on the blackboard. "Anyone missed anything?"

"I got your collar size ..." started Willie.

"Clam up," snarled Jumbo. "Okay, Adam. Take over."

Adam had been sitting, quietly. His black face was contemplative. His computer mind had absorbed, analysed and interpreted the facts presented by his friends. He didn't look up. His voice was soft. The men leant forward in order to hear his words.

"Five women, Jumbo." Adam lifted an eyelid so he could glimpse Hooligan's face while he made this observation. His chief didn't react. "Five women," Adam repeated. "First, Ulysses got only woman smell on the plinth. Unlikely that one woman would change her talcum or perfume so often. So there HAS to be more than one woman. How many? Five. Five it is, because it would take that many to move the pelvis. It had to be women—not small men. They had no mechanical expertise—they tightened some nuts while trying to loosen them. The tools were badly chosen. A man would have made certain he'd got good quality wrenches on a big job like this." Adam paused, consulted his mental notes and continued. "They used the canvas over the dinosaur as a tent. A good touch, that. They slept and lived there part of the time. The rubber smells are air mattresses—two of them, doubles. And they ate while they were there. They came and went in the daytime, when the museum was open, and worked only at night. Had to, because of the painters. They dismantled everything, then moved it out in one go."

Adam looked up. "Is it okay if I start guessing, now?"

Jumbo Hooligan smiled. "I like your guesses, boy," he said. "Go ahead."

Adam guessed. "Five women. I can't be certain of their ages. Remember that flake from a teenager's shoe? And one of them knits ... she's more likely to be elderly than a youngster. Certain things, like the tea, and at least two types of perfume, suggest European women. I'd make a serious guess that they were Limeys. Very few other Europeans like scented tea, and the Earl Grey tea is typical of elderly upper-class British. At first, I thought it was maybe a gang of those dames the English call debs—you know, society dolls with nothing much to do but annoy everybody. But things didn't fit—society dolls don't wear coarse stockings, or cheap nylon tights. Then it all clicked ... the baby powder. D'you remember noticing how the nuts and bolts taken off the frame had been neatly piled out of the way? Unlikely a man would do that. So, what sort of women do we have in New York who are mostly elderly, have European society tastes, are possibly British and who spend a lot of time with babies and who are used to putting things out of harm's way? My answer, Jumbo, is ... children's nurses. So that's my bet: five dames—nannies, and British."

Jumbo Hooligan leant back against the edge of his desk, and smiled delightedly. "Great sleuthing, Adam," he said. "That's a lead I can really use." He tossed the stub of chalk into the box beneath the blackboard, and looked at McGraw. "Boots, you get me the names of all British aliens registered as children's nurses who are working in New York."

He pointed at Ulysses and Willie. "I want you two guys back at the museum. Find out if they've spotted any nannies around there recently. Then check out with Two-O precinct. It's their beat. Maybe they'll have something we can use. Now, the rest of you ..."

Willie Halfinch interrupted him. "Boss, that single nipple print's been bugging me. I got an idea. Maybe one of the dames was dressed in a wrestler's leotard."

*   *   *

Boots McGraw turned in his report at Jumbo's office after lunch the next day.

"Help yourself to the squawkbox," smiled Sheba. "I'll get some coffee."

130

"Hi, Jumbo," Boots said into the intercom. "You want me in there?"

"Sure," replied Jumbo's voice. "And tell Sheba to send in the others as soon as they arrive."

"Okay, Chief," called Sheba, from the coffee machine in the corner.

"Here, let me take it," said Boots. He took the two plastic cups, and backed himself through the door into Jumbo's office. He put a cup in front of Jumbo. Then he produced the list given to him by the British Embassy.

"Eighty-six British broads registered as children's nurses, Jumbo. I got all the details. Looks like a lot of hoof work, but I guess ..."

Jumbo's intercom buzzed. He flicked it. "Ulysses and Polyphemus," said Sheba.

"Thanks for the culture, Doll. Wheel 'em in." He looked expectantly at the door. "Hold on," he said to Boots. "Want to hear from the others, first." He swung his feet down off his desk and twisted his swivel chair to face Ulysses and Willie as they came through the door. "What d'you get?" he asked.

"A homer, Jumbo," replied Ulysses, as they settled themselves in the yellow armchairs. "Listen to this. Willie and I covered the museum, like you said. They said no, they hadn't particularly noticed any children's nurses behaving suspiciously, but sure, they'd seen quite a lot about. They were always in there with their kids. Zero, okay? Then we slid over to Two-O Precinct and ran the rule over them. We came up with this. A few days ago, an Englishman died on the museum steps. He collapsed. The British Embassy claimed his body. Don't know the autopsy report yet, or any more details about him. But what we DO know is that there were two children's nurses—British—with him when he died. Coincidence, huh?"

Ulysses produced a slim pad from his pocket, and glanced at it.

"Their names—Hettie MacPhish and Melissa St. Clair.

We checked them out of their apartments and followed them for two hours this morning. I think they're our lead. The young one—she's some dish—called for the one named MacPhish. She didn't have any kids with her, and there aren't any at the address she uses. But the old dame works in a family with children, and she brought one with her when they came out."

Willie's excited voice broke in. "We followed them down to Central Park. Eight hundred and forty-two paces, from the old dame's apartment to the park."

"Sure," Jumbo said, wearily.

"They met some other nurses, on a seat, by the Alice statues," continued Ulysses. "They made five, altogether. And that's where we got stumped ... at least, a little."

Jumbo raised his eyebrows.

"Not too much," said Willie, hastily. "It was just that there was only two of us—and two into five ain't much good when it's people you're following. So when they split up, at lunchtime, Ulysses and me were only able to follow two of the others, to find out where they lived. There's one more yet to go."

"So who've we got, so far?" asked Jumbo.

Ulysses replied. "We've got the two original dames, and the two new ones. Their names are Emily Biddle—she's kind of old and odd—and a middle-aged one called Una Nesbitt ... about forty, maybe. The one we couldn't tail was about eighteen."

"Not much we can be sure of yet," grunted Jumbo. "We're not even a hundred per cent certain about the number of people involved in the robbery. Could be quite a different group."

"We've got that print," said Willie, brightly. "All we've got to do is to check them against it."

"Say, Willie, that's great! I'd forgotten that." Jumbo winked at Boots McGraw. "Okay, Willie, you go and get the nipple dabs of all five dames, then we'll match them against the one we've got on file. Right?"

Willie Halfinch flushed with pride.

"Okay, boy, what you waiting for? Beat it!"

Willie left the room.

"Jumbo!" chided Boots. "You gone crazy?"

*   *   *

Willie walked down the corridor away from Jumbo's office. He was grinning to himself. It was his first solo assignment as an agent. He squared his shoulders and pressed his left elbow into his side. He could feel his gun in its holster. He felt good.

He stopped in the corridor opposite the lift and looked at the indicator panel. The elevator was on the ground floor. Willie eyed the call-button. Glancing left, then right, along the corridor, he stood himself a yard away from the button. A look of concentration was on his face, his legs were slightly apart, his hands dangled at his sides. Suddenly, he moved. His right hand flashed under his jacket. He crouched. The hand came out again, filled with pistol. Willie hit the call-button with the nose of the barrel—first time. He grinned in satisfaction as the lights showed the lift was on its way up. A sleek young secretary wiggled her way round the corner and down the corridor. He winked at her. She ignored him. Willie grinned even wider. He didn't mind the snub. After all, the girl didn't know about him—yet; Willie Halfinch, the Special Agent. He flexed his muscles and pulled in his chin. The lift arrived. The doors opened. Willie ducked his head inside.

"Down, bud," he said abruptly to the liftman.

"Sure, Willie, down. You got the hump, or something?"

"Nope," snapped Willie. "Busy."

"Big job?" asked the liftman. Willie squared his shoulders again and stared straight ahead.

The lift stopped. Willie strode out through the entrance hall, barged aside the green glass doors, Hooligan-fashion, and stood, straddle-legged, at the top of the steps. The grim expression on his face slowly faded into blankness.

Gee, thought Willie. Nipple prints. How the hell am I going to get their nipple prints? He wondered if it would be possible to rummage through their linen baskets, in search of discarded underwear. No good, he decided, you wouldn't get prints on fabric. His brow furrowed. If the broads were young, and they were sunbathing face-down on a tiled swimming pool surround, maybe he could sneak up and pull off their bikini tops. That'd get him a print on the tiling, which he could dust down afterwards. Useless—it'd be washed away by the time they let him out of jail.

Willie sagged.

Suppose he disguised himself as a girl, and waited until they got undressed in a dress shop? He shook his head. No guarantee that would work, either. Steel discs sewn into the cups of their bras? He shook his head again. They'd notice the cold metal. Ahhhh—metal, that was it! Maybe if he hired a suit of armour ... ? Nope. How the heck could he get a strange nude dame to embrace him in a battle-can? A survey, maybe? Suppose he went along with some printed forms and said he was from a medical firm. He shuddered. He could picture himself saying—"Morning, ma'am. I'm a representative from United Aspirin. Doing a survey, ma'am. Want to ask you something personal." She'd nod, and say, "Go ahead." Willie gulped at the thought of putting his next question—"Ma'am, d'you mind if I check your chubbies?"

Willie turned slowly around and walked hesitantly back into the building. The lift was still waiting.

"Up," said Willie.

"You got sick?" asked the liftman, looking at the worried Willie.

Willie shook his head.

He put his hands in his pockets and strolled out of the lift and back down the corridor towards Jumbo Hooligan's office. The sleek young secretary wiggled towards him again. This time she smiled up at him.

"Hi!"

134

"Yeah," grunted Willie. The secretary pouted and walked on.

Willie passed through Sheba's office and knocked quietly on Jumbo's door.

"Come in, Willie," roared Jumbo's voice. Willie gulped and stuck his head round the door. "Yeah?" asked Jumbo, hiding another wink at Boots.

"Er, Boss," stammered Willie. "I've been thinking . . ."

"And about goddammed time," roared Jumbo. "Come back in here, sit down, and shut up."

*　　　*　　　*

Jumbo's entire team sat in the seats in front of his desk. It was their late evening conference. He surveyed them. Willie felt himself blushing again, and was glad when Jumbo's eyes moved on along the row.

"You start, Adam," said Jumbo.

"The hooks are in," replied Adam. "I've checked the Central Park patrolmen. You know, the cop-on-the-beat stuff. Often works. They've seen these dames hundreds of times. Seems they're always there together. Always in the same seat at the same time of day. Known to the horse patrolmen and the scooter boys. Got something useful from one guy. Says he noticed a couple of times recently that the dames WEREN'T on their usual bench. Seems they're so regular in the fine weather he can check his circulating time by their arrival."

"It's still pretty thin," said Jumbo.

"Not quite so thin. I got wool fibres from the seat they use. Same type, brand AND colour, as the stuff Boots got in the museum."

"Ahhhh," breathed Jumbo. "That's more like it."

"As I say, Jumbo. The hooks are in."

Jumbo Hooligan whistled through his teeth. "Right," he said. "I want these broads tailed and checked every minute of the day." He looked at his watch. "You may not score tonight. But tomorrow make like you're their shadows."

8

Simone was sitting up in her carriage—and hating it. She preferred lurching about in the grass of the park, and sitting, examining bits of dirt, some of which she found edible. She reached over the side of the carriage and grasped her neighbour's feed bottle. The neighbour objected. Simone belted him between the eyes with his own lunch. Then, with sudden cunning, screamed agonisingly, even before her pained and surprised enemy had time to react to the violence. Almost immediately, she regretted her outburst. She was heaved into the air, swung around and dropped, breathless, on to her tummy. A heavy adult hand whopped her rear. "Old soldiers never die," croaked the Scots voice. Simone kept quiet. She'd learnt that the sooner she relaxed, the quicker she'd be back in the safety of her carriage.

Una folded her airmail edition of the *Daily Telegraph* and stuffed it under the pillow of her baby-carriage. She turned to the other nannies sitting alongside her on the park bench.

"Whoever it was who borrowed that dino . . . Sassenach thing has caused quaite a dreadful commotion," she said. "All that simply frightful newspaper publicity."

"Randy says the thieves'll get thirty years' jail when they catch them," added Melissa.

Emily's knitting needles clicked to a lower gear. She held up the latest of Tarzan's waistcoats and examined it. "Nobody will arrest them," she announced. "All they've got to do is to keep calm, and act normally. Remember, no one's going to suspect THEM." She shook the knitting, then tucked her elbows into her waist as the needles gathered speed again.

Una sat primly, her hands clasped on her lap, her ankles neatly crossed. She watched the passers-by. "There are a lot of people around in the park today."

Fifty yards away, sitting on one of the smooth heaps of rock, was Ivor. He was watching Melissa, and was playing Scrabble with the Russian agent delegated to shadow him. The Russian agent was cheating.

"Hey, are you sure there's such a word as . . ." Ivor scowled and tried to pronounce CKZWG.

"Certains, mine ver goot fren," replied the Russian. "Mine aunt caughted it."

Willie Halfinch was wearing a park-keeper's uniform. He was carrying a pointed cane and had been spiking bits of paper. He was embarrassed. He'd accidentally impaled a French letter and was trying to remove it without any of the nannies noticing. A yard and a half behind Willie trundled the stout figure of Pi Wun Tun, disguised as a Haitian immigrant, wearing dark glasses and a flowered shirt, and studying a copy of the Quotations of Mao Tse-tung. He was so engrossed with his reading that Willie twice had to ask him to stop bumping into him.

Susanne was watching Ulysses Pilgrim. He lounged at the foot of an elm tree, wearing a poncho and a pair of tatty jeans frayed around his ankles. His feet were bare. He was softly playing a guitar and humming to himself. Through half-shut eyes he was watching Susanne. She was a pretty little girl, the sort of girl, he thought, he'd be happy to shack-up with. He'd read about English roses—and this was a real English bloom.

Ulysses was also being watched by Pierre, the French agent. He watched Ulysses, Susanne, and the Chinese agent. The French agent was disguised—as a British agent. He liked to think this subterfuge caused confusion. It would have done, but the Frenchman always blew his own cover. He couldn't resist patting, petting or pinching every girl's bottom. No Englishman would behave so indiscriminately. He was commonly known to Hooligan's mob as the French Tickler. They always knew how to find him. They just listened for the sound of a face being slapped. The French Tickler's complexion always seems to glow with rude health.

The German agent wasn't even there. He was in hospital. On the previous day, he'd been ordered to make contact with his boss in the middle of a public swimming pool. With true Prussian phlegm he'd plunged into the ten feet deep water to make the rendezvous. He hadn't heard a word of his briefing. He'd spent the entire interview underwater, drowning. Adolf Krautbukket couldn't swim.

Krautbukket wasn't worried. For, the next day, he'd just bribe one of the others to fill him in on the latest details.

Hettie was being watched by Huw. And Huw, in turn, by a freelance Italian who worked on spec for the Japanese. The Italian had a personal vendetta with the Russian agent and was wearing a bullet-proof vest. It weighed twenty-seven pounds. His face was puffy and mottled. He was wondering if he were about to get heat stroke. He was praying that he wouldn't have to move.

"A clean pair of heels," Emily waved her knitting, on her needles, like a psychedelic banner. "That's what THEY'VE shown them. I told you they would. Nothing to worry about. It's finished. Just the packaging and posting to do."

Emily noticed the military-looking man with the ginger hair. He looked like a retired officer. He was sitting on one of the seats a few yards away, reading the business section of the *New York Times*. Boots McGraw had punched a pinhole in it, and watched Emily with infinite attention and a squint. On the base of the Alice Memorial opposite sat a Greek. He watched McGraw. Boots knew he was there, even without looking. The Greek was always there. Boots McGraw and the Greek had an understanding. They weren't sure what the understanding was, but it had been that way ever since the Greek had sent McGraw a bottle of Ouzo on St. Valentine's Day. Boots'd had it analysed. He'd felt cheated to find that it wasn't poisoned. It made the Greek spy seem unprofessional.

*   *   *

It was six in the evening, and Jumbo Hooligan was angry. He wasn't in the park. He was in his office bathroom. Until today he'd believed that this was the only room in his suite where he could find privacy. Now, he was removing a small bugging device from the lavatory pan.

"That bloody French Tickler," he growled. "It must be. Nobody else would bug the john."

He thought of the bugging attempts of the past few years. The English had probably been the most gentlemanly. They'd inserted a transmitter into the spine of a book of etiquette, and in turn slipped the book, beside the hundred or so other training manuals, on Hooligan's bookshelves. Jumbo had been insulted at the time. Not so much by the bugging device, more by the unsubtle hint.

The Italians had blundered. A new agent made the mistake of bugging Hooligan's wastepaper bin. The next day, three of the Italian spy team were sent home, suffering from perforated eardrums.

The Cuban attempt was artistic—and very nearly a success. They had Hooligan's office portrait of a nude repainted on a copper printed circuit. Miniature batteries were hidden in the picture frame. Unfortunately, their artist used plastic paints, and the gentle warmth of the printed circuit caused the picture's breasts to droop and grow in length. As the picture was the first thing Jumbo Hooligan's team looked at when they entered his office, it was soon spotted.

Petrov, the Russian, had bugged one of the small knobs on the television receiver. Hooligan found it at once. With sadistic glee, he'd spent a joyful afternoon playing back, through the device, the confessions of a Soviet defector.

The team of Chinese spies had been the most annoying. They'd bugged everything. It had taken Jumbo and his team two days to clear the office of a hundred and thirty-five transmitters. They were in everything. Jumbo had been furious and hadn't spoken to the Chinese since.

Jumbo Hooligan knelt in front of the lavatory pan, trying to ease the small cartridge out of the lip of the porcelain. A voice boomed close to his ear. He jumped.

"Hey, Boss." It was Willie Halfinch. "Gee, oh, gosh. Er, you want a help out, Mr. Hooligan? Hey, fellas, come and give a hand. Mr. Hooligan, he's fell down the pan."

"Get out," screamed Hooligan. "Get out while I'm working. Wait in the office. And damn well knock in future." He pulled his fist out of the pan, shook it free of water, and stuck it under the tap on the washbasin.

"Now you've done it, Willie. He'll be mad as hell for hours." Huw Schwartz drew his finger across his throat. "He'll have your head. One thing about Jumbo . . . he don't like to be disturbed in the john."

Hooligan stamped into the room, rolling down his shirt-sleeve.

"Right . . . who got anything?"

Huw looked tired. He shook his head.

"Nothing?" blazed Hooligan.

Huw was silent.

"But they must have done something!"

"We picked up the four whose names we've got as they left home this morning. They led us to the Alice Memorial. They met the fifth one there, a young blonde chick, called Susanne. That's all that happened."

"All?"

"Sure. Just the normal nurse-type behaviour. They sat on a bench. Took the kids to the playground, came back and sat again. Went to their apartments at lunchtime, and returned to the same park bench afterwards. Scolded the kids a bit, played a few games with them, went to their

140

apartments again at around five o'clock."

"They didn't speak to each other while they were in the park?" asked Hooligan.

"Yeah, they chatted," replied Huw. "But we couldn't close in on them. Those dames have got hawk eyes. You should see how quickly they notice when their small fry get out of line."

"Okay," said Jumbo Hooligan. "Now we know some of their routine, let's try again. This time we'll use a directional microphone. Not everybody. Just you, Willie. You try one. Get one fitted into your cane—ask the technical boys."

*　　*　　*

New Yorkers wanting to make a telephone call from the three phone boxes outside the Plaza had been avoiding the centre booth for several days. It stank. Complaints to the telephone company brought the usual quick action. They cleansed, disinfected and fumigated—to no avail. It still smelt like a charnel house. The manager of the Plaza even considered having his hotel jacked up and rolled a few yards further away.

In the Tse Eih Aei headquarters below, the stench was even worse.

"Another one," panted Nicky Po, staggering in from the sewer tunnel and hurling a limp, three-foot alligator on to the floor. Fat Choy sighed through his surgical mask. He reached over, grabbed the dead reptile by the tail and dunked it in a bucket of salt water. Then he expertly skinned it. "We've got enough meat to last us two months," he said, tossing the carcase back into the sewer. He hung the new skin alongside the others on the damp wall.

"Here's the alum." Sam Ling tossed him a round container. Fat Choy caught it, and rubbed the powder into the hide. "How many's that?"

"Forty-seven, Comrade Ling," answered Fat Choy, tears from his smarting eyes soaking the gauze of the mask.

"And when will the skins be sufficiently cured?" asked Pi Wun Tun.

"By November," said Fat Choy, balefully.

"Then we'll have them all ready for the Capitalist mid-winter gift-giving festival?" said Chou-Tan.

Sam Ling sighed. It would take a lot of time to replace the money lost in the fire engine incident. He didn't think Lui Ho's scheme to manufacture hundreds of wallets for Christmas out of the alligator skins was the quickest way.

The door of the sewer headquarters was pushed open, and Lui Ho walked into the room. He held his nose and waited as the steam condensed on his glasses. He wiped them dry, then turned to the wall photograph of Mao Tse-tung, and saluted.

"Where id de fake dragon?" he demanded, nasally.

"We tailed the nanny-ladies all day," Sam Ling told him. "They didn't go to the resting place of the fake dragon. What is even stranger, they didn't even mention the hiding place."

"Den we will capture one, brig her here, and extract the idforbation. Todight!" snarled Lui Ho. "You, Fat Choy, you will brig id one ob de naddy-ladies, de youg one." Lui Ho smirked and took a new hold on his nostrils. "Her figger dails are do doubt of adbirable legth to be gripped by a pair of pidcers. And," he added by way of encouragement to his team. "We shall find out afterwards if what dey say about Occidental women id correct."

"Hooligan," said Sam Ling, quietly.

Lui Ho's face bleached to a paler shade of yellow as his hand dropped from his nose. "Hooligan?"

"Hooligan," repeated Sam Ling. "HE knows. The park was crawling with those running dogs of his."

"He is protecting the nanny-ladies?" asked Lui Ho.

"Watching them."

"Watching them? Then it would seem there may be things happening between the British and the Americans that we do not know about," said Lui Ho. "Possibly the

Western powers are in great disagreement. It may even be possible that the British and the Americans are planning to declare war on each other."

"I will volunteer at once, in such an eventuality," said Pi Wun Tun. "I will join the British Grenadiers as a general."

"Most admirable sentiments," said Lui Ho, thoughtfully. "But, much as I enjoy such enthusiasm for war against the American capitalist society, the point now is that our present work is made more difficult by Hooligan's interest in it."

"Not so, Comrade Leader," said Sam Ling. "As the Americans say, every cloud has a silver lining. None of us doubts our ability to succeed in this venture. So, when we triumph, so much greater will be the discredit and humiliation falling on that dog's head Hooligan. His revealed inefficiency will earn him execution. And our future work will be easier."

The spies smiled. Lui Ho nodded agreement. "So!"

Sam Ling continued. "We carry on as before, to your original plan, Comrade Leader. We wait for the right opportunity. Then we will employ a cunning stratagem to distract Hooligan and his pig-pack long enough for us to get the fake bones away, back to our glorious Motherland."

"Magnificent," hissed Lui Ho. "Such ignominy for Hooligan! Such disgrace! We will carry on, then, just as though he does not exist."

"A great shame," whispered Chou-Tan, quietly. "The interesting conundrum concerning Occidental women must, for the moment, remain unanswered." He sighed deeply.

*   *   *

"I think Her Majesty will like this," smiled Emily, in the park the next morning. She examined a crumpled sheet of wrapping paper, printed with miniature Father Christmasses. It rustled in the breeze. "I've brought plenty with me."

143

Hettie leant forward and peered inside Emily's carrier bag. "It's ALL Christmas paper," she said.

"Yes, I save it. It's so cheerful. I never throw ANY away."

"We cannae wrap the Sassenach bones in that. It's most improper. Remember, they're going to Her Majesty."

"Tish, tosh and rubbish," said Emily. "I never mind getting presents in used wrapping paper. It's a sensible economy." She pulled out another piece of paper and smoothed it flat. "Look at this bit—fairies and gnomes. And it's got tinsel stuck to it."

"We'll buy a few rolls of brown paper," Hettie said. Her old friend looked hurt. "Och, all right, lassie. We'll use your paper on some of the smaller pieces."

Further along the bench the three other nannies sat quietly.

"The park seems crowded again today," remarked Melissa.

"Must be a mid-week festival. Garibaldi Day, or something," said Emily. "Americans are *always* holding them. I saw one last week. D'you know, they were actually commemorating the invention of the pre-packed loaf!"

Una sniffed. Her eyes were watering. "Something that nobody has noticed. All the people. They're men."

Hettie looked at her in surprise, then stared round, suspiciously. She recognised a Haitian-looking man who seemed to spend a lot of time standing in the undergrowth, close behind the tall park-keeper. The park-keeper was collecting paper again, but today he seemed to be having trouble with his cane. He kept lifting it and looking at the end. Many of the other men were also somehow familiar. Hettie noticed that none of them looked directly at the nannies. This, in itself, was suspicious—men usually looked at Melissa.

Hettie decided to try an experiment. She collected her belongings and whispered to Emily, "Back in a minute." Then she loosened the brake on her baby carriage and slowly wheeled it down the path. From the corner of her eye, she watched two of the men begin to move with her. She wheeled the carriage farther. The men followed. There was no doubt about it. The first man to move took great care she shouldn't notice he was following her. It was the second man who attracted her attention. He was very obviously following the first man. She did a circuit of the lake and wheeled the carriage back to the others.

"Dinnae look up," she hissed out of the side of her mouth to Emily. "Those men are all watching us. They must be policemen. Pass the word along to the others to follow us, and not to talk." Hettie wheeled her carriage away again, trailed this time by the other nannies. Emily caught up with her.

"Where ARE we going?"

"Just come along, lassie. We'll explain in a moment," said Hettie.

She led the way until they arrived at a spot near the open air theatre, then she stopped.

"Right, set the prams in a circle round us," she ordered. The nannies arranged them like covered wagons awaiting an Indian attack. Then they sat together in the centre of the ring. The men slowly wandered into view, but didn't approach too closely.

"Now," said Hettie. She reached into Emily's carriage and shook the baby, sharply. There was an immediate noisy protest from the enraged Lindon. The other perambulators provided a descant. The nannies were surrounded by a wailing wall.

"What on earth?" protested Una.

"Let them cry. It does them no harm. And we need the noise. Those men, they're definitely following us. And that park-keeper has got a microphone or something in his stick. We've read about them. He's pointed it at us several times."

"Who are they?" asked Susanne, worried.

"They must be police," replied Hettie. "We thought we'd got away with it. Somehow they're on to us."

"Why don't they arrest us?" asked Una.

"Obviously they cannae be certain."

"They're pretty persistent, these New York police," said Melissa. "They'll keep on until they get what they want. They'll find out."

"Och, they won't find out," said Hettie. "If they knew for certain they'd have arrested us. They're just trying to force us to make a move. We've got to keep our nerve. We left no clues in the dinosaur hall. We cleaned up everything. They're probably following everybody in New York at the moment. We dinnae have to worry. Remember Miss Emily's advice: just act perfectly normally. If the men talk to you, talk back. Dinnae be frightened. And if anyone questions you, about the business, just deny any connection with it. If we all stick together, they willnae be able to prove a thing. What we've got to do now is fix our alibis."

It took them fifteen minutes to perfect their cover-stories. At last, they were satisfied.

"Whatever happens, dinnae alter them," warned Hettie. "Stick it out to the bitter end."

"And the bitter end it's quaite likely to be, too," said Una. "If we're caught, they'll throw us into jail and then deport us. It'll be in every English newspaper—the *News of the World*, *The People*."

Emily brandished her knitting, like a small flag. "We won't be caught. Nanny Hettie's quite correct. But if we are—" she gave the knitting flag another waggle—"remember one thing—we did it for Great Britain AND Her Majesty, God bless her." She looked at them, fiercely. "I'd gladly go to prison for my country." She puffed out her chest, until Susanne thought the starched pinafore would crack.

"As the 25th Earl himself would have said, 'Hear, hear'," added Hettie.

*　　*　　*

Jumbo Hooligan was whittling. It was intricate work. He
146

held a new pipe-stem on his blotting pad and shaved a sliver of wood from it with a razor blade. His team sat in their armchairs and watched him. He fitted the new stem into the corncob bowl and grunted approval, then he tapped it home firmly on the side of his desk.

"Right," he said, wedging the repaired pipe into the corner of his mouth. "Adam's come up with something hot. The Limey who died on the museum steps was a British Intelligence agent. He was playing mailman with a pickup from Hawaii." He removed the pipe and scratched the side of his throat with the mouthpiece. "Now for some real bad news. The information he was carrying has international classification of Red-Stripe-Red. And it's missing."

"Jesus, Boss," said Boots.

"Yup . . . Jesus," repeated Jumbo. "And that's what the guys at the top said when they heard."

"What's Red-Stripe-Red, huh?" Willie whispered to Huw, sitting next to him.

"Any information that could involve the West in war," said Huw, quietly.

"Jesus, Boss," said Willie. Jumbo Hooligan glowered at him.

"The Limey agent was the Earl of Hastings. Sort of royalty, almost. He was supposed to make his handover inside the museum. But he died before making it. The British Embassy say there was nothing on his body when they checked it. And he was poisoned."

"Poisoned?" queried Ivor.

"Yeah, with his own pill."

"Could have been an accident," suggested Ulysses.

"Not over-likely," said Adam. "He was an experienced operative. And there's something else, all the previous agents in the delivery chain from Peking were killed just AFTER they'd made their pass. And the last man in the link has disappeared. Seems he didn't collect from this British Earl. Somewhere along the line I guess the Reds caught up."

"Reds?" Willie looked surprised.

"Chinese Reds," said Adam.

"So the dames are Chinese agents?"

"Maybe, Willie; maybe not."

Hooligan slapped the bowl of his corncob on his palm. "So this is how it reads. The Limey Earl dies on the museum steps, on his way out. He hasn't made contact with his buddy, yet the message isn't on him when the embassy check later. Two of these Limey nurses are with him when he collapses. Then the dinosaur disappears. What does that add up to?"

Hooligan surveyed his team. "Pretty clear what happened, huh? God, we've gotta find those bones. I'm pretty damn certain they AND the message are still somewhere in the city."

"It's still being combed, Jumbo," said Adam. "The precinct boys are checking buildings, derelict lots and parks. But it's a big city."

Jumbo twisted his pipe between his fingers. "We don't have much time. Those bones are going somewhere, and somebody is anxious to get them away fast. We've got to get to them first. Adam, check the background of all those nurses. Get me something solid. See if either of the old ones did any missionary work in China before the war!" Hooligan paused. "One more thing, the Big House gave me a message it wants passed on to you: Find that Red-Stripe-Red . . . and get that dinosaur back, or we'll ALL be on display in the museum."

"Don't worry, Boss," said Willie, kindly. "They couldn't really do that. Remember what President Jefferson said." Willie pushed himself up from his chair and stood to attention. "All men are created equal, that they are endowed by their Creator with certain unalienable Rights, that among these are Life, LIBERTY and the pursuit of Happ . . ."

"WILLIE . . . SIDDOWN," roared Jumbo.

Huw waited until the echo had died round the room. Then he spoke. "Say Jumbo, d'you figure we could pull 'em in and charge them on the evidence we got in the museum?"

"Baby, in that museum we got nothing. Nothing at all. All we got were clues to identities. But facts? No. How d'you think it would look, with great blue-chinned lawmen like us trying to nail an espionage charge on some innocent-looking old ladies with baby-buggies parked in the court-house aisle? With what for evidence? A couple of hairs, a few strands of wool, some complicated smells, baby powder, and a nipple print. Yeh! A nipple print! Not a chance. We got to have facts. Copperbottomed facts." Jumbo gave in to temptation and leapt at the wastebin, booting it hard against the wall. It flattened itself in a muffled and metallic explosion. His team winced.

Hooligan shuffled the squashed paper-bin with his toe. "We're dealing with Limeys, and we all know what that means. If we hooked a charge on them, with that sort of testimony, they'd ice up and bluff it out."

Ulysses looked up at Hooligan. "Boss, I think these nurses know we're tailing 'em. They didn't spot us, but they couldn't miss that spy circus outside."

Hooligan grinned. "Good! Then let's pressure them a little," he said. "We'll tighten the screws even more. Make it obvious we're on to them. Tail 'em closer, boys. Try to scare them into action. Maybe if we put the squeeze on, one will talk."

"What's your meaning, Boss?" asked Willie. "You want we should beat them up some? I couldn't cream a lady. My momma would never forgive me."

"Jerk. Not beat 'em up, just worry them a bit. Split them. Bring them in for questioning. But, remember, treat them real gentle. And be polite. They're British citizens, don't forget. We don't want an international incident."

Hooligan looked over at Ulysses. "On the way out, ask Sheba to call Two-O Precinct. Tell them we want to use their station house for the job. I'll meet you all there in half an hour. Each of you pull in the broad you've been shadowing." He dismissed them with a brief nod and a wild kick at the flattened bin.

"Hey, boss," said Willie, as he reached the door. "You wanna know something?" Hooligan lowered his eyebrows, fiercely. "What?"

"Judging by the impact damage, I estimate your bin's doing 37.8 miles an hour when it hits the wall. This means that the energy you expend is enough to . . ."

"Piss off," roared Hooligan.

9

Getting the whole of Pi Wun Tun's tubby figure into the spin-drier proved difficult, even with the combined efforts of the Tse Eih Aei team.

"Why don't we just put the top half inside?" suggested Fat Choy.

Pi Wun Tun ducked his head into the opening, while the spies pushed from behind. His shoulders jammed solidly against the sides of the round hole. They pulled him out again. He wiped a hand across his sweating forehead.

"We're doing it for your own good," said Fat Choy.

"Then remember you're NOT going to terminate me. It's ONLY corrective treatment ... a LITTLE corrective treatment," pleaded Pi Wun Tun.

"If you try to get inside it yourself," said Sam Ling, eyeing the stout figure of Pi Wun Tun, and the narrow opening of the machine, "we'll put it in the records as a course of self re-education."

Pi Wun Tun sighed, removed his shoes, and pushed one leg into the spin-drier. "I don't suppose it'll help much if I apologise again?" he asked, hopefully.

"No," said Lui Ho. "Now stop farting around and get inside. I have enough objection to your reading lurid and obscene capitalist literature, but to hide *New York Nudes At Night* inside your autographed copy of the Quotations of our beloved Mao . . ."

"The treatment is only for five minutes, anyway," said Sam Ling, consolingly.

Pi Wun Tun wriggled his leg farther inside. "You'll have to help," he groaned. "I can't lift BOTH legs off the ground at the same time." The other spies held his shoulders as he forced his second leg into the drum. "Now push me." For several minutes they pushed. Pi Wun Tun gradually disappeared into the spin-drier. Only his head remained outside the door. "No good," he said. "That's all of me that will go inside."

"Start the motor, then," Lui Ho ordered. The spies felt in their pockets for quarter dollars to feed the machine. They shrugged. "Obstructionists," screamed Lui Ho. "Hasn't *anyone* got a quarter?" There was silence from his team.

"I have," said Pi Wun Tun obligingly, his head protruding from the spin-drier like that of a French aristocrat lashed to the guillotine, "but in my trouser pocket."

"Sometimes, I wonder how our beloved country tolerates so many imbeciles," moaned Lui Ho.

For once, Sam Ling was in complete agreement with his Comrade Leader.

*　　　*　　　*

The Cuban, Russian, Greek, Italian, French and German spies were already cluttering the 20th Precinct Station House steps by the time Jumbo Hooligan arrived. He noticed the Chinese was missing.

Hooligan waved the agents aside, and ran up the steps, two at a time. An invisible, but audible, barrier stopped him just outside the door. He froze. He wished he'd remembered to tell his team not to bring the children along with the nannies.

Hooligan hesitated, then strode determinedly inside. The front office was in chaos. To his right, on the pale-green desk, sat a young lieutenant, his legs dangling. He held a screaming child, face down, across his knees and was singing, in a youthfully toneless voice, something about old soldiers never dying. He tapped the infant's bottom smartly in time to the rhythm.

Ulysses Pilgrim's feet stretched out into the centre of the room. He lay, slumped, on a chair. His head seemed to be distorted. His right eye was already a bright purple. There was a line of blood running down his lips, from his nose. The youngest of the nannies was repairing him by winding yards of four-inch bandage enthusiastically round his forehead.

Another nanny seemed to be suffering from convulsions at the side of her baby carriage. She sat and heaved, her eyes streaming, continually sneezing. Her children added to the noise with piercing yelps.

The red-headed nanny was having a shouting match with Ivor. As Hooligan watched, she stepped back and clipped him on the ear. Huw, on the other side of the room, jumped, put his hand to a smarting ear, and yelled "Lay off" to his twin.

Just in front of the radio officer, an elderly nanny was breathing fire at a young and very timorous policeman. He was leaning backwards against the desk, trying to get farther away from the infuriated woman. She poked her face close to his. Hooligan again couldn't hear the words, but there was no doubt the young patrolman could.

To his left, on a bench, sat the oldest of the nannies. She seemed to be oblivious to everything. She was calm amidst the hurricane of noise and confusion, and was quietly knitting some rainbow garment, while her baby, in its carriage, leant over the side and banged the ancient central heating radiator expertly with a policeman's nightstick.

Jumbo Hooligan looked. The noise was appalling. The

off-duty cops were standing in the corridor to their rest room, watching. Hooligan stared at the sign he knew was pinned just above the door. It read: 'Please be considerate to our neighbours. Be quiet at all times.' He winced.

"SHUT UP . . ." he bellowed. No one even heard. He tried again. "BE QUIET." His voice was lost in the wilderness of sound. He remembered a piece of his early training, lowered his voice to a normal speaking range, and said, "Okay, everybody, please quieten down." There was silence. Faces turned to look at him.

He opened his mouth to speak. And pandemonium was stirred up again.

"QU-III-ET," he stormed. Again there was silence. He spoke, rapidly, to take advantage of the moment. "Okay, let's get some order into this meeting. You . . ." He pointed at the nanny who had the policeman pinned against the desk. "You, ma'am. I'd like a few words with you. Please come into the office."

Hooligan turned to the others. "And try to cool it in here." He opened the door to the Deputy Inspector's room and ushered in the indignant nurse. He started to speak to her, but she interrupted him.

"Look here, my good man. We dinnae know if you realise that we're a British citizen and a subject of Her Majesty. You have no right to hold us here without reason."

Hooligan tried to speak again.

She cut him off. "Don't try to bamboozle us with pitiful explanations," she thundered. "We want the truth, man! Our Queen will hear of this. You can't try these high-handed tactics with Hettie MacPhish. We've tanned more respectable hides than yours. Royal bairns' backsides. And we can do the same for you."

Jumbo Hooligan looked round for the second person. He decided she was schizophrenic. He was amazed at the amount of words she could get out in one breath. She began again.

"And who are you, anyway, ma laddie? Where are your

credentials? We demand to see the British Ambassador at once. We used to be Nanny to his nephew. And what about our bairn? It's way past her feeding time. How DARE your men lay their disgusting hands on our person? Well, come along. Tell us."

Hooligan tried.

"Sorry, ma'am. I just want to . . . er, I want to ask . . ." Hettie interrupted him again.

"For God's sake, laddie, speak up. Dinnae mumble."

Hooligan stuttered. "I, er. My department. We're just trying to clear up a few . . . er details."

Hettie seized on the word.

"Details?" Her nose flared in anger. "Details? You must be a wee bittie daft. You dare to bring us here to discuss details? How DARE you? Bring us here to discuss details, indeed. You and your whole department, must be mad."

Hooligan put his hand on the woman's arm. It was a sad mistake. She hit him swiftly with her handbag.

"Take that, you common lout. Lay a hand on a British citizen? Assault a lady, would you?" She hit him again. Jumbo Hooligan backed away.

"Police," screamed Hettie. "Police. We're being assaulted. Police!" She hit Hooligan for the third time. He backpedalled as fast as his bulk would allow.

"Villain," shouted Hettie. "Fiend. Help . . . POLICE!"

Willie Halfinch burst into the office, his pistol in his hand.

"Good God, no," shouted Hooligan. "It's me, you fool. Get this crazy hen out of here. Release her. Tell her to go home." He thought for a moment. "No, don't tell her to go home. Take her . . . Drive her home."

Willie stuffed his gun back in its holster. "I ain't got a car, Boss."

Jumbo Hooligan fumbled in his breast pocket. He pulled out a ten dollar bill and threw it at Willie. "Then get her a taxi." He thought of her schizophrenia. "Two taxis, if she insists. But, GET HER OUT OF HERE."

Hettie poked her chin in the air, shrugged her uniform

more comfortably on to her shoulders and peered down her nose at Hooligan. "And not before time, ma laddie."

As she stalked through the door, Hooligan heard her order Willie: "First, get us some warm sterilized milk from your canteen. It's way past Simone's feeding time."

Jumbo Hooligan slumped in the Deputy Inspector's armchair, pulled out a handkerchief and wiped his face. He eyed the Inspector's wastebin, but didn't have the energy. It took him a full quarter of an hour to calm down. The noise outside continued. At last, he stood and walked over to the door.

A patrolman, swinging his stick, lumbered up the station house steps and into the muster room. He began to edge himself through the noisy crowd. Hooligan noticed him. He remembered his name only because the 20th Precinct claimed he was the ugliest cop in the city.

"Porcello," called Hooligan. The patrolman looked round. "Over here," shouted Hooligan. He decided that the men of the 20th Precinct were right. Vittorio Porcello had been ugly even before he'd become a boxer. He'd started off with an overlong nose, this had been squashed flat over almost half his face in his twenty-seven straight fights as a professional. He was regarded by his officers as the reincarnation of Neanderthal man, and was in great demand in quelling student riots. He terrified them.

"Uhuh, Mister Hooligan, sir," said Porcello, lumbering closer. "You want ME?"

Jumbo Hooligan smelt the garlic from five feet away. No wonder Porcello was surprised to be called.

"Yeah. Help me out, will you? Bring me that woman over there." Hooligan pointed across to Una, still sneezing on the bench. Porcello nodded. Hooligan went back into the office.

Seconds later, Porcello led Una in. She collapsed, gratefully, into a chair.

Jumbo Hooligan tried his calmest approach. He walked softly to her side and put his hand gently on her shoulder.

155

She heaved an enormous sneeze.

"Lady," he began. He was stopped by another sneeze. "Lady . . ." he began again. She sneezed even louder.

"Ooops," she gasped, and sneezed again, her eyes watery and her cheeks damp with tears. "Sorry, I . . . ah . . . tishooo."

"Lady!" Hooligan tried a third time. "I only wanted to . . ." His question was drowned by two quick sneezes. "For God's sake, lady." Hooligan looked at Porcello, who shrugged.

"I guess it must be some sort of 'flu, sir."

"That's all I need," said Hooligan, timing his words to correspond with the shortening gaps between Una's sneezes. "Look—lady—I—got—some—questions . . ."

"Beg pardon," gasped Una. "Can't talk. Quaite allergic. Impossible. Aaahtishoo . . ." She stifled the sneeze in her wet handkerchief.

Hooligan sat heavily on the edge of the desk.

"Take her outside again," he told Porcello, resignedly. "Get her a drink of something. I'll see her later."

He followed them out and looked around. He caught sight of Pilgrim, holding his heavily-bandaged head in his hands.

"Ulysses!" he called. "Come in here. I want to speak to you and the girl."

The battered Ulysses eased himself out of the chair with the help of Susanne's arm around his waist. Hooligan waited until they had entered his office, then he shut the door behind them. He swung round suddenly.

"Now look here," he roared.

The teenage Nanny blanched. Jumbo Hooligan was satisfied. This one would be easier than the others. She could be broken.

Ulysses raised his one good eyebrow slightly.

"Look here," Hooligan roared again. "I've had enough of this. I want the truth. And now." His face was so close to Susanne's she could feel his breath on her cheeks.

"The truth," he demanded, his face even closer. Their noses were almost touching when she bit him.

"Herough . . ." shouted Hooligan, jumping backwards so quickly he stumbled over the chair. He clutched his nose. It was bleeding.

"I'm frightfully thorry," said Susanne, politely, "but I thought you were going to attack me. Daddy told me the best thing to do when attacked is bite. Does it hurt much?"

"Hurt!" yowled Hooligan through fingers held against his bleeding nose. "Assaulting the law. I'll have you in for life."

Pilgrim looked at his boss, sympathetically.

"I got it both ways, Chief. I went to pick her up, like you said, and a young Central Park cop thinks I'm assaulting her. So he works me over with his prod. I try to stop him, an' she joins in. McGraw's Greek spy saved me."

"I'll kill her," blazed Hooligan. "Get her outa here. Get them all outa here."

The nannies stood in a group outside the 20th Precinct Station House. Hettie looked satisfied.

"Did you say anything?" she asked Susanne.

"Nothing, but I bit him."

"Wonderful, wonderful," said Una.

"Yes, wonderful," congratulated Emily.

"Really too wonderful for words," said Una, again.

"For heaven's sake, woman," snapped Hettie. "No need to keep repeating yourself."

Una looked at her, dreamily. "It's so wonderful," she said.

Hettie shook her by the arm. Una jerked, and blinked. "It happened," she said. "It's happened."

"What?" asked Melissa.

"I didn't sneeze at him," said Una, pointing up the steps at the ugly Porcello, standing guard at the entrance like a gargoyle. "He didn't affect me. Look." She ran up the steps and pushed her arm through Porcello's. He looked astonished. Una smiled. "See, no sneezes."

"Amazing," said Hettie.

"Absolutely amazing," said Emily, squinting through her pince-nez.

Melissa looked at Porcello. "Poor Una," she said.

Jumbo Hooligan stood by the office window, looking at the bunch of nannies, and their carriages, below in the street. He walked over and shouldered the office door shut. He scowled at the wastebin. It was square and heavy. He stomped over to it. Gave it a moment's contemplation. He considered the fact that it belonged to someone else, then leapt into the air and delivered a drop-kick at it. There was a sharp, audible crack and a cry of pain. Hooligan flopped untidily onto the floor beside the still-intact bin. He looked down in horror at his ankle. It had a strange mis-shapen look about it. He suddenly felt sick. There was no doubt it was broken. The cast-iron bin had barely moved.

*　　*　　*

There were two plasters on Hooligan—one at each end. The one across the tip of his nose made him slightly cross-eyed. He raised his head and looked at the white cast round his ankle, swinging uncomfortably from the scaffolding at the end of his bed.

"It's a delightful fracture," the surgeon said. "Most intricate and complicated . . . quite rare. Everyone's interested. Kept a set of the X-rays, myself."

"How long?" asked Hooligan, in a bored voice.

"Dear man, what a worrier! No time at all. Absolutely no time at all."

"And HOW long is no time at all?"

The surgeon remained professionally cheerful. "Oh, about three months," he laughed.

If Hooligan had been fit and well, he probably would have leapt across the ward and flattened a wastebin.

"Tough," said Adam, from beyond Hooligan's suspended leg. "Real tough. And just when we thought we were getting somewhere. But I guess you can still brain it from here."

Hooligan thought cautiously before he spoke. You didn't make too many mistakes in front of a bright second-in-command like Adam.

"I've been thinking it over," he confided. "Those dames don't react like normal people. They're nuts. We'll have to try a different approach."

"I guess we ought to, too," said Adam. "Last time we tried everything but rubber hoses. They're a strange bunch, all right. I haven't found out much about them so far, but the British Embassy are getting background details from England. We might get a lead eventually through Porcello. He made a hit with the nurse who's allergic to men. Seems he's the first man she's ever met who didn't make her sneeze."

Jumbo Hooligan looked sideways out of the window, and watched the red tugs working in the river before he replied.

"I still think we might be able to make a deal with them. Maybe I should try again. Get me the crazy broad I didn't interview. She's the oldest. Maybe she's the leader."

Adam pushed a small, decorated box towards Hooligan.

"By the way, here are some more chocolates, Jumbo. We've cleared this one. It's okay—from Petrov, this time. That makes fifteen boxes you've had."

"Fourteen," corrected Hooligan. "And if I ever lay hands on that bloody Lui Ho, I'll stuff his laxative-laced ginger up his Chinese fanny."

*   *   *

Emily stationed herself just beyond Hooligan's plastered foot. He smiled at her. With the plaster on his nose he reminded her of one of Hettie's teddy-bears. She half curtsied.

"Sorry to hear about your inconvenience, sir."

"Hurumph," replied Hooligan. His foot and nose continued to ache. "I want to talk about this damn dinosaur." He tried to keep his voice soft, his tone reasonable. "Look, lady. The time has come for you and me to have a little chat. We know you knocked it off."

He noticed Emily's look of horror. "All right, don't get touchy. We've got all the proof we need to get a conviction —and I ain't kidding. We've had you followed every minute of the day, for some time now. We know ALL about every one of you . . . Don't interrupt me, lady. D'you know I can get you sent down for life? Get me? LIFE? So, we make a deal. You tell us where the old brontosaurus is, and I'll try to be nice and easy with you. Now, I'm a reasonable guy . . ."

Emily broke in. "Oh, dear me. How embarrassing for you, Mr. Hooligan! Do you REALLY believe I could steal a dinosaur from a museum? After all, it's such a big thing, isn't it? I do have an idea, though. Perhaps I CAN help you."

Jumbo Hooligan strained forward as far as his leg harness would permit. Emily bent over him and whispered. A despairing groan escaped from Hooligan. He sank back against the pillow. "All nuts. Nuts. Completely nuts," he gasped, banging himself on his forehead with the palm of his hand.

"No, *really*. I mean it," continued Emily, confidentially. "My friend lost her canary. And within two hours of advertising in the *New York Times*, she had a lot of people telephoning her wanting to sell her a replacement. Perhaps you can get a dinosaur that way. I don't suppose the museum people would spot the difference. After all, a dinosaur's just a dinosaur."

Jumbo Hooligan jerked himself upright in the bed, swore as his ankle gave him a painful reminder of its condition, and fell backwards on to the pillow.

"Right," he hissed. "I've tried to be generous. Now I'll tell you something. I'm going to re-open Alcatraz for you. You'll all spend the rest of your lives inside. In solitary. And when you do get out, then we'll deport you—in boxes."

"That *will* be nice!" said Emily. She picked up her

handbag, twitched her pince-nez back into position, and smiled again. "Do have a nice LONG holiday, Mr. Hooligan."

10

Something stirred amongst the stocks and shares. They rose and fell rapidly. Billie Big Canoe opened a dew-heavy eyelid and squinted down the bristles of his chin towards the financial section of the *New York Times* that had kept him warm throughout the night.

Maritime Motors seemed to be reaching a peak. He was a little worried about Amalgamated Faucets, whose market price had remained static for the past month. He inhaled deeply—not that he needed the extra air. It simply enabled him to read the remainder of the column without bringing his hands out into the morning freshness.

Billie Big Canoe was a financial expert. He spent more time studying the stock market than looking for work. After a few minutes of careful reading he pulled a tatty notebook from his pocket. More fumblings produced a tooth-marked pencil stub. He flicked through the pages, crossed out a few figures, and made a quick mental calculation.

Since March he had made financial gains of over a million dollars. If he'd had the initial thousand dollars for the original investment, he would now have been a millionaire. As it was, Billie Big Canoe didn't have the price of a hamburger.

"How's the market today?" asked Herman's voice from the next bench. A strange couple, Billie and Herman. They had little in common, although they had travelled together for nearly twenty years. Their interests were divided, as a result of sharing the same bedclothes. Every day they searched for a copy of the *New York Times*, and every evening, they split it. Billie took the financial and news pages, and had become a stock market expert. Herman preferred the sports and social columns. He knew all the socialites by sight and name, their comings and goings, intrigues and scandals.

Billie answered out of courtesy. "Market's good. The dollar's up. How's the rest of the world managing?"

Herman peered down over his chest. "Nothing much. I see that Hazel Willingboddy has screwed off to Italy again with that new gigolo friend of hers."

"Uh huh," grunted Billie Big Canoe. He found the antics of Herman's socialites boring.

He stood up, crumpled his newspaper into a ball and tossed it behind the bench. Then he stretched and rubbed some life back into his arms and legs.

Herman's shirtfront heaved, and a glistening, scaled coil popped into view. Euclid, his pet python, was trying to force its way down the dark leg tunnel of Herman's old jeans. Herman tugged—the snake won. He let go of its tail and the snake emerged by the side of a grubby ankle. Herman caught the python, wrapped it around his neck, and stood up.

"I got him," he smiled to Billie Big Canoe. "He's only making trouble 'cause he knows it's coming towards winter. He wants to find somewhere hot."

"Why the hell you got to have a snake as a pet? A dog, yes . . . but, for God's sake, a python! Doesn't do anything, except make a darn nuisance of itself."

"Well, it ain't got fleas, either." Herman stroked Euclid's sleek head. "And I didn't choose it, anyway. It got given me."

Herman was the world's most unsuccessful bum. Euclid was a scaly reminder of his luck. Herman had knocked at a tidy suburban house. The woman had smiled at his 'got anything you don't want, lady?' She'd returned to the door a few minutes later with a bag, and handed it to him. Herman heard the door being locked, then he'd seen the bag move. It had taken a lot of courage to look inside, even more to handle the snake. He'd intended to sell it, but then decided to keep it as a pet. Now it lived around his neck during the daytime, and under his clothes at night. Herman was the only friend it'd ever had.

"Put it away, I said, and let's go see Albie for some coffee."

They plodded into the city. It was still too early in the day for the morning rush of commuting New Yorkers. Herman spotted a lone, well-dressed man, document case under his arm, striding along the avenue towards them. He intercepted him.

"Say, mister. You got change for a five thousand dollar bill?"

The man shook his head.

"You spare us the price of a coffee? Just till the Chase Manhattan opens?"

The man felt his loose change, found a coin and tossed it to Herman. Herman beamed a toothy smile. The man grinned back—it was that sort of a bright morning.

They drifted to a broken-down timber shack on the edge of a building lot, and stayed till gone noon, swigging coffee with Albie, a renegade hobo now working as a site guard. They smoked the last of the cigarettes they had bought with the money they got from the man with the briefcase. Then they ambled slowly downtown. At the corner of Fifth Avenue and East 42nd Street, a voice, harsh with Brooklynese, stopped them.

"Goddam me," exclaimed the cop. "You two bums still cluttering my beat? Why don't ya head south with the boids? New York's gonna be tough this winter."

"We been thinking about it, Joe," said Billie.

The cop looked them over.

"Say, youse guys eaten, yet?"

"Nope," replied Herman. "We just had coffee."

"Here, then." The cop put his hand inside his tunic. "Have these. My Nellie always gives me blutwurst. Can't stand it any longer," he lied, and tossed them the flattened package he'd been looking forward to having for his own lunch.

"Now, on your way!" he added, eyeing Billie and Herman with exaggerated and theatrical anger. "Scram offa my beat. And don't lemme see youse around again till next spring. 'Cus if I do, I'm gonna shoot ya."

The three of them laughed. It was a laughing afternoon.

*　　　*　　　*

By early evening, the two hobos had reached the edge of the East River. An autumnal haze blurred the lights from across the river and dusted the scene blue-grey.

Herman nudged his friend. "Whatsay we head over to Welfare Island and find a place to bed down? The old buildings there should be warm."

"That's good, by me," said Billie. He thought of the damp of the previous night. "Fall's coming fast. Coupla weeks and we'll do like Joe said, and head south."

It was almost dark by the time they'd strolled over the Queensboro Bridge and made their way down on to the Island. They avoided the main paths and the porters and guards around the hospitals, and followed the riverside towards the derelict buildings. Billie eyed them, professionally. The first ones he rejected as too damp, draughty or uncomfortable, but he stopped in front of one which seemed to be in a habitable state.

"Here," he said, and nodded towards the door. It was jammed. He barged it with his shoulder. It opened. Inside it was already dark. He trudged in. There was a heavy clump. "Take it easy," he called back. "This place is full of lumber."

Herman followed him. There was the sound of a striking match. Billie Big Canoe held the flickering splinter of waxed cardboard above his head.

"Jesus! Bones! This must be the mortuary we're in."
The match died. He struck another.

"These ain't people bones," said Herman. "These are too big. These are animal bones. Hey, I bet these is elephant bones. Maybe this is one of those elephant graveyards yuh read about. You know, where they come to die . . ."

"You're nuts. You think sick elephants is going to swim the Atlantic, just so's they can die on Welfare Island? Maybe some film company left them here. Maybe they're something the students used when this was a proper hospital. Maybe even someone left them to the laboratories in their will."

"Hold Euclid, while I get out the candle, will ya?" Herman unwound his pet and dangled him at Billie.

Billie stretched out his hand and waved it around until he felt the snake. It was even more unpleasant in the semi-darkness.

"Hurry up," he groaned. "This damn thing's cut off my circulation."

Herman searched through the few belongings in his ex-army rucksack and produced a bent stick of tallow. He lit it.

They looked around. Billie found himself a tattered mattress that was disintegrating in the hallway. He pulled it over and kicked it into a rough bed shape.

"What we got for supper?" asked Herman. "I was fancying a steak, fried, but rare. And two eggs and tomatoes and mushrooms, and maybe even some wine—at a table with a clean cloth on it."

"Well, we got half a blutwurst sandwich left and two apples."

"Joe the cop was right," said Herman. "That blutwurst's lousy."

"You ain't got no gratitude." Billie tossed him an apple and part of the half-sandwich.

"You know, pal," Herman sighed between mouthfuls, "I've been thinking. That Hazel Willingboddy . . . a dame like that. She's got everything . . . I mean that. That Hazel

Willingboddy's got the lot. Jet-set. Money. Big hotels. Clothes. You know, I never seen a picture of her wearing the same clothes twice. I bet she changes her pants every day."

"Nuts," snapped Billie. "What for you're always on about that broad? I hear that dame's name twenty times a week." He dragged over one of the bones and settled back, in almost armchair comfort, to read his newspaper. The candle glimmered, its yellow glow adding an antique varnish to the men's skins.

"Hey," he said, suddenly excited. "These bones, Herman. These bones, are they stone or bone?"

"Whatdya mean, is they stone or bone? What you think they'll be, marshmallow?"

"No, jerk. I'm serious. Have a feel of one of them bones."

"Now who's nuts?"

"Give it a dig with your blade."

Herman pulled out his old knife and tried scratching the nearest bone. He looked surprised.

"It IS stone . . . These ain't bone bones at all. They're concrete. Must be part of a statue. Maybe we can sell them. Billie, you're a genius! Maybe we can sell them to a collector, maybe an antique shop."

"We can do better than that, buddy." Billie jumped to his feet and, pushed the paper in front of his partner's face. "Throw a look at that bit on the right. If I ain't wrong, it's these bones they're yakking about. It says dinosaur bones. And there's a reward. Says the museum'll pay 10,000 dollars. And we've got 'em here. Jeez, ten grand!"

"They'll think we stole 'em," warned Herman. "The cops will toss us inside. You can stake your life we won't get a reward. They don't give rewards to bums."

"Nope. This is legit. It's a museum. They'll pay us a reward."

"How we let 'em know it was us who found the bones? If we leave here, maybe someone else'll find them."

"We gotta telephone them. I gotta telephone them and

you gotta stay here on guard."

"It's night time," said Herman. "Nobody important's going to be at the museum at night. And we don't have a dime between us—for the telephone."

"Oh, Jesus," groaned Billie. "We got ten grand sitting waiting for us. And all we need to get it into our hands is a goddammed dime. Okay, we sit here until it gets morning, then I go see 'em."

Billie looked at the pile of bones that now represented a fortune to him and his partner.

"Whatcha looking like that for?"

"Nothing," replied Billie. "Just thinking."

"Thinking about the money?"

"Sort of."

"Whatcha mean, sort of? Now you're looking at me real funny. Like you just seen me for the first time."

"I was never so close to 10,000 dollars before. And I just looked and decided what a scabby hobo you really are. I don't even know if I can trust you to watch the bones while I'm away at the museum."

"You've trusted me for twenty years."

"Yeah, but not with my money," said Billie. "You'll have your share in your pocket about three weeks and then you'll be round at my penthouse, bumming from me." He glowered at Herman.

"I know what it'll be like. You'll fritter it away like a foolish virgin—high livin'; drinks on Herman; gold collars for your snake. How else d'you expect me to look at you?"

Billie Big Canoe stared at the pile of bones, now twenty-four carat gold in the candlelight.

"These bones is our Klondike, and we don't want any other bums muscling in, so we gotta keep guard. And we don't want the cops finding them, either." He blinked, suddenly. "God, Herman. Blow out that light. Fast."

Herman blew. The light died. "Hey, Billie," said his voice from the darkness. "How am I going to stay awake all night?"

"Keep guard—like we was in the army."

"But, Billie, when we WAS in the army, we used to sleep on guard. Remember?"

"Dry up, bud," commanded Billie. "And stay awake." His mind was already working on a sensible investment system.

They woke simultaneously at midday.

"You cheated on me," Billie scowled. "I told you to stay awake and you slept." He looked round, hastily, to make sure the bones were all there. The pile looked dusty and worthless in the misty light that filtered through the old windows.

"I never slept," lied Herman. "You slept. I watched you."

"Like you watched my ass," said Billie. "Okay, anyway, they're here. And so are we. Lemme look at that paper again."

"How we going to tell the museum?" asked Herman.

"I'll walk over. And you stay here. You guard the bones." Billie's voice became threatening. "You move an inch outa this place, you let one hobo in here and I'll gut ya. It's going to take me a good while to hike over there."

"They won't believe you," said Herman. "They'll think you're on the bum. How'll you make them believe you got the bones here?"

"I'll take one with me." Billie looked round and selected the smallest vertebrae. He wrapped it in the newspaper and tucked it into his shoulder bag.

"Don't let them cheat you," warned Herman, suddenly frightened. "You remember them twenty years? Okay? You remember we been equal partners for a long time?"

"Sure—equal partners of nothing," said Billie. "Now we got something, I guess it don't make any difference." He kicked open the door and looked cautiously outside, as though expecting an ambush. "Don't forget. You move outa here and I'll fillet yuh. I'll be back." He pulled the door closed behind him, and began the long trudge across town.

* * *

The museum official was signing mail. He was tired. It had been a long and tedious day. His secretary knocked and stuck her head round his office door.

"There's a strange man down in the hall who says he wants to talk to you."

"It's too late to see anyone now," said the official.

"I told him you wouldn't, but he said you'd want this parcel." She held out an untidy package of newspaper.

"What is it?"

The girl shrugged.

"Better open it. Probably something he wants identified."

The girl unwrapped the package. The official continued signing his mail. He glanced up. The girl was standing, her mouth open, staring down at the pile of paper.

"Well, what is it?"

"You'd better look."

He looked.

"My dinosaur!" He picked up the bone and fondled it lovingly. "Get that man up here, FAST."

Billie was shown into the office.

"Cigarette? Cigar?" The official held a box towards him.

"Thanks," said Billie. He took one of each. He lit the cigar, and put the cigarette in his pocket for Herman.

"Well?"

"Your dinosaur," began Billie. "The paper yesterday wrote there was a reward."

"Yes, yes, of course. There's a reward, but first we've got to get the dinosaur back."

Billie wasn't taking chances. "Put it in writing that you'll give ME a reward if I show you where it is."

"It's already in writing."

"Put it in writing that Billie Big Canoe gets 10,000 dollars. Then I'll show you where it is."

"I can't do that," said the official. "Don't worry, you won't be ... er ... chiselled if you really show us where the brontosaurus is."

Billie got up. "Goodbye," he said, and started to walk

169

towards the door.

"Come back," called the official. "Okay. I'll give you a letter, saying you were the first to bring me the information."

"No dice," said Billie. "You just write an I.O.U. for 10,000 dollars from the museum. That'll do me. I don't want no fancy stuff. I'll show you the bones, you give me the cash."

The official sighed and pressed a buzzer on the desk. His secretary reappeared.

"Type me a letter, promising to pay Mr. Billie," he looked over at the hobo. "Mr. Billie who?"

"Big Canoe."

"Just saying that we promise to pay him the 10,000 dollar reward AFTER he takes us to the dinosaur."

He looked across at Billie. "Okay?"

"Okay," said Billie. "You got a truck? We need a truck."

"Yes. Excuse me a moment." The official picked up his internal phone and dialled the Department of Vertebrate Palaeontology. He was excited. "I've found your dinosaur," he shouted into the instrument. "Meet me at the car park, with a truck and a couple of men, in five minutes."

*   *   *

"It's five o'clock. Time we were away," said Hettie. She stood like a sergeant major in front of the other nannies. "Everybody here? Everybody ready?" she asked.

"Everyone," replied Susanne.

"How many children?"

"Just three babies," said Una. "Dear Mr. Porcello's looking after the others."

"Och, you HAVEN'T left them with HIM?" asked Hettie, incredulously.

"Why not," said Una, peevishly. "He's VERY responsible. And kind. *And* he's a policeman. Policemen often look after children."

"Exactly! He IS a policeman; what on earth does he think YOU'RE doing, lassie?"

"I told him I had to go hospital-visiting," said Una. "He's quaite happy, watching television. Anyway ..." she smiled smugly ... "I think it's quaite a good thing that he's learning about children."

"Una, you're behaving like a thirty-eight-year-old teenager. We wish we were as confident of him as you are," Hettie stiffened. "Right, let's get on with the job. How many carriages?"

"Two," said Melissa.

"Then load them into the lorry. Tie them to the sides, so they don't rock about."

"I've brought some more pretty wrapping paper," said Emily, wedging a small package behind the wheels of one of the carriages.

"Got plenty." Hettie pointed to a large roll already inside the truck. "Everything we'll need. Paper, string, glue, sealing wax, adhesive tape, marking pens, scissors, torches and lamps. All we have to do now is to wrap the bones, then load the parcels into the truck. Tomorrow morning, we'll take them to the post office."

Emily closed the truck doors, walked round the side and climbed into the driver's seat. She waited until Hettie had settled herself. The Scots nanny looked across at her.

"Clean your spectacles first, Nanny Biddle."

Emily polished her pince-nez on her skirt, then clamped them back on her nose.

"You may commence driving," said Hettie. "And keep an eye open in case we're followed by the police."

*   *   *

Lui Ho held the metal rail in front of him. His face and hands were blurred and his voice warbled with the vibration of the Tse Eih Aei's latest transport.

"R-r-r-remember-r-r-r," he strained to get the words out coherently. "Th-a-a-t if-f we loo-oo-se the-e-e na-ah-ahny--lay-ay-dies this-s time, you-oo wi-ill be il-il-um-ilim-alo ... execu-uted," he panted.

Sam Ling muttered and pressed his toe even harder on

the gas pedal. The Tse Eih Aei garbage truck swung out of the side road, fifty yards behind the nannies' vehicle.

"Such realism," sighed Nicky Po, standing on the bouncing footboard at the rear, and sniffing at his reeking overalls.

Pi Wun Tun pulled his cloth cap down over his eyes, and pushed aside one of the dustbins hanging on the truck, before he answered. "For such realism, there should be a reward," he muttered. "Perhaps the award of a thousand long-horned beetles."

"A thousand long-horned beetles? I haven't heard of that," said Chou-Tan. "Is it a new honour?"

"Very," said the barely reindoctrinated Pi Wun Tun. "I just invented it. The thousand long-horned beetles should be stuffed up Lui Ho's rearmost orifice."

Nicky Po rolled his eyes upwards. "Without doubt, our Comrade Leader has excelled himself today. To think that I studied in a People's University for five years in order to qualify for a place on the footboard of a capitalist garbage truck!"

*　　*　　*

It was dusk by the time Emily drove her truck on to Welfare Island. It bounced over the rough ground, lurching and swaying. Inside, the nannies held each other for support.

"Take care, woman. Good God! STOP," Hettie shouted as the truck rumbled towards the river. Emily swung the wheel, wildly.

"Sorry, my spectacles fell off." She steered the truck towards the derelict building and parked beneath the trees. "It'll be safe and sound and out of sight here," she said.

Hettie turned to the nannies in the back. "Troops, outside. We've arrived."

They climbed down into the long grass at the side of the track.

"The children?" asked Emily.

"Asleep," replied Una. "The bouncing quaite exhausted them."

"It made ME sick," said Melissa. "I don't think I've ever

172

been in such a nasty lorry as this one. I felt sick the first time as well."

"I liked it." Susanne rubbed her hand over the dirty glass of one of the building's windows, and peered through. "My goodneth, Nanny Hettie, I think there's thomeone inside here."

"Where? Let us see." Hettie pushed Susanne aside. "Good God. A man. Looks like a tramp. And he's asleep on the bones." She squared her shoulders. "Let us go in first. We'll soon settle him." She stamped into the building. The other nannies waited.

"Geroughhh ..." There was an odd sort of explosion inside. The nannies waited. A small cloud of dust drifted out of the doorway. They heard Hettie's strident voice haranguing the man. Seconds later, he stumbled on to the path. He saw the other nurses, gulped, raised his cap and scurried off into the undergrowth. Hettie appeared at the door, brushing dust off her skirt.

"All clear now," she called, gaily.

Susanne turned to Melissa and whispered. "What d'you think she did to him?"

"Don't ask," warned Melissa. "At your tender age, it's best you don't learn about such things." She looked at Susanne's puzzled face. "For heaven's sake, girl ... what d'you think she did? Disembowel him?"

"Inside, lassies," order Hettie. "There's a lot of work to be done. Susanne, you bring in the paper and things."

*   *   *

The Tse Eih Aei garbage truck lurched on to Welfare Island with a clattering jerk that snapped Lui Ho's teeth together like an old-fashioned mousetrap. He rubbed his jaw and pointed towards the parking space in front of the new hospital buildings. "The nanny-ladies went down the other way. We'll stop here and follow them on foot."

Sam Ling eased off the accelerator until the truck was trickling forward at only a couple of miles an hour. Out of the corner of his eye he watched Lui Ho open the door and prepare to climb out. Then, when he'd calculated Lui Ho's head was in a suitable position, he stamped on the brakes.

Lui Ho's forehead ricocheted off the cab roof and slammed against the windscreen. He slumped on to the seat, his eyes watering, his wire-rimmed spectacles crazed like old ice on a skating pond.

Sam Ling smiled the sort of Oriental smile that Westerners mistake for a blank look. "So sorry, Comrade Leader," he apologised. "But let me congratulate you on almost perfect self-control, spoilt only by a slight intake of breath towards the end of the calamity. Forgive my ineptitude at stopping capitalist waste disposal vehicles."

"What's going on?" came Pi Wun Tun's voice from the rear footboard. "You stopped too quickly, and Comrade Chou-Tan's fallen in the garbage."

Sam Ling climbed down and strolled round to the tailboard. Chou-Tan was brushing small particles or rubbish off his shoulders. Sam Ling wrinkled his nose.

"This is the downwind side. Come over here," Pi Wun Tun said cheerfully.

Lui Ho, his eyes straining behind his cracked glasses, clambered out of the passenger seat and felt his way along the length of the truck to the back, where he could hear his men talking.

"Silence," he growled. "And you'd all better listen carefully. If there's any slip-up tonight, then the person responsible gets SPECIAL correction." He tried to ignore the pain from his swelling forehead. "You will carry out my orders at once, and without comment. You, Fat Choy, in the truck you will find two anti-tank rifles and a flamethrower. Bring them here. We will then hide ourselves in the bushes till the time is right. When I blow my whistle, we will ATTACK in the manner advised by Chairman Mao—in two waves. We three, without guns," he indicated Sam Ling and Fat Choy, "will follow in the second wave, and will pick up the weapons of you who have fallen in the cause of true Communism. The Imperialist nanny-ladies will be eliminated. We will then radio the submarine, which will cruise up the river and collect the bones. By tomorrow morning, they will be well on the way to our glorious homeland."

"And we will be conveyed, just as speedily, to Sing-Sing Penitentiary," said Sam Ling, flatly. "I have no doubt whatever, Comrade Leader, that our superior fire-power and military audacity would achieve victory over these nanny-ladies. However, the danger would also be present that such a confrontation would attract unwanted attention to us BEFORE we could load the fake dragon bones on to our submarine. There is, in addition, one further complication. It is well known that the American coastal radar system is totally inadequate, and that foreign submarines can sail, unhindered, up to the East River. But I am sure, Comrade Leader, you will admit that not even a People's Republic submarine, manned by the world's most enthusiastic and best-trained submariners, armed with the Thoughts of Chairman Mao, can sail up a river which is devoid of water —and full of fire engine. Unfortunately, you see, the tide is out." Nicky Po and Pi Wun Tun sniggered. Sam Ling continued. "Humbly, I submit that now is an excellent opportunity to apply the old American proverb 'softly, softly catchee monkey', and your previous and most brilliant plan suits the circumstances admirably."

"It does? For a moment, it slips my accursed memory," said Lui Ho.

"Yes, Comrade Leader," Sam Ling chose his words carefully. "You suggested we should secrete ourselves until we were certain as to what the nanny-ladies were doing. Then, you wisely advised, we should wait until they left, and, in the darkest part of the night, we should remove the bones to a new hiding place. Later, you said, we would take the bones thirty miles out to sea in a fishing boat, in the early morning mist, and, avoiding the United States

175

war-mongering patrol boats, radar and aircraft, rendezvous with our submarine."

"Of course! I remember now," said Lui Ho, to Sam Ling's relief. "That's the plan I intended you to carry out." He paused. "But what did I suggest we should do if the nanny-ladies take any of the bones away with them?"

"Ah," breathed Sam Ling, his mind working like a motorised abacus. "You said that, in such an eventuality, we were to follow and hijack the bones the moment they left them unattended. Wisely, you ordered that our glorious Bureau must never be suspected of involvement."

"Of course," smiled Lui Ho. "That is the brilliance I have learnt to expect from myself. For, if we reveal ourselves to the nanny-ladies, the dung-fly Hooligan may learn of our interest. Up to now, his imbecilic investigations have been limited merely to the disappearance of the fake dragon. We must not draw his attention to the espionage implications." His smile widened. "And now, dear comrades, to fill the dull moments of our waiting, I propose to read you a small and apposite portion of the Quotations of Chairman Mao."

*   *   *

Billie Big Canoe was enjoying his ride in front of the museum truck. He grinned to himself at the thought of three well-dressed New Yorkers travelling in grubby discomfort and sitting on piles of old sacking behind him.

"Head for Columbus Circle," Billie told the museum official. "Now down East 59th." He issued the route a few blocks at a time. He wasn't convinced he could trust his companions.

"Keep ahead. Over the bridge. Now take the elevator down to Welfare."

"Of course," breathed the official. "The old hospital buildings."

"Okay," said Billie when the lift had lowered them to the island. "Follow the river. Hey, wait a minute!"

A scruffy figure darted out from behind a bush and began to run. Billie yelled out of the window.

"Herman! Herman, you crumb!" The figure stopped, and turned. "Herman! You just come back here." Billie swung himself down from the truck. "You crummy bastard. What you doing running away like that? I left you on guard."

"I was on guard," stuttered Herman. "Gee, Billie, I *was* on guard, but some crazy nurse came along and told me to get out of the hospital grounds. I waited around 'cus of the money. I thought you was more hospital people."

"Nurse?" said Billie.

"Nurses. Lots of them. They're still inside. They scared Euclid. Maybe we made a mistake. Maybe them's hospital bones, after all, not dinowhatsit bones."

"What's going on?" called the museum official.

"Nothin'," said Billie. "Just that my buddy got frightened by some skirts. Your bones are safe. Come on, I'll take you to them."

* * *

"It's where?" Jumbo Hooligan sat up in bed, yelped with pain as his ankle jarred, and glared at Adam. "Ulysses followed them on a motorcycle he borrowed?"

"A speedcop's 'sickle," said Adam.

"He loaned it to Ulysses?"

"Not exactly," said Adam. "We'll have to square it, later. Ulysses reports Lui Ho's Reds are in on it. Six of them in a garbage truck."

"The hell they are," growled Hooligan. "I've been waiting for those bastards to step out of line. Now I've got them. Loosen off that cord." He pointed towards the support holding his leg. "I gotta get out of this goddammed bed. Can't do a thing from here."

"For Christ's sake, Jumbo. You'll spring your fracture again. I'll handle the job. I can get the boys down there and sort it out."

"Nope." Jumbo Hooligan clamped his jaw. "This is my hunt. I want to be there at the kill. Get Sheba ..." He winced again. "Get her and say I want a chopper on the roof here in half an hour. And tell the doctor that I've got to get out. If he's worried, tell him I'll be back in a couple of hours."

"You're crazy, Jumbo. But, okay, I'll fix it."

"And warn Two-O Precinct. Tell them that my team is heading for Welfare Island. I want the whole place sealed off. Stop all traffic crossing the bridge. Keep a path through for our cars. Break out the special equipment and fix up roadblocks. Don't let anyone on, or off, the island."

"Okay, boss." Adam turned by the door. "Gee, you're a wild bastard."

"Nurse," roared Hooligan. "NURSE!"

A frightened young Sister trotted in.

"Get me a wheelchair. And I want to get on the roof." He took a deep breath. "AND PRONTO!"

*　　　*　　　*

They winched Jumbo Hooligan, in his shiny chrome wheelchair, into the helicopter. Half a dozen medical orderlies sweated and heaved. A posse of worried doctors and nurses watched.

"Hurry up, damn ya," shouted Hooligan. The pilot pulled the chair backwards into the cabin. "You," screamed Jumbo, pointing at the broadest of the orderlies. "You come along. I want a pusher."

The orderly swallowed and climbed aboard. The rotors sputtered into life. The nurses' skirts flapped as the helicopter lifted into the dusk. It climbed quickly and headed towards the East River. Hooligan bellowed loud instructions to the pilot, clamped on headphones and buckled a throat microphone into position. He looked down. The evening lights of the New York traffic seemed a long way below. The aircraft started to drop towards the Queensboro Bridge.

Hooligan was ahead of his team. The home-going New

York traffic had slowed them, even though their sirens blasted a path. The precinct police were already there. Hooligan watched them flagging down cars. He spoke into his radio.

"Where are you, Adam?"

"Be at the bridge in a few seconds," replied a static-crackling voice. "We can see the roadblock ahead."

Hooligan looked down the approach road to the bridge. He could see his team's car lights flashing. He spoke again into his microphone.

"Okay, okay. Check with the lieutenant and make sure he's got the island properly sealed." As he looked down, he could see Adam's car stopping alongside the police barrier. He watched his deputy open the door and run to the officer standing by the bridge rails. A moment later, Adam called him on the radio.

"Everything okay down here, Jumbo. The bridge and all approach roads are covered. The river police boats are deployed. The island's watertight. How's the leg?"

"Doing better than my stomach," said Hooligan, as the helicopter dropped another few feet. "Right, start the men moving in slowly. Get all the searchlights trained on to the island."

"Hey, Chief ..." Adam's voice, metallic through the radio, was startled. "I can see a flashlight, and men outside one of the buildings—and a truck."

"Get the boys in close, and line up the arcs. We'll swing the chopper round and drop onto the car park at the other end of the island. We don't want to wise them up. Let me know when you're 'go'."

Hooligan bit his nails until Adam called back a few minutes later. "All ready, Chief."

"Get me down." Jumbo signalled the pilot, and pointed to the ambulance park. He tensed his muscles as the helicopter dropped, like an express elevator, towards the concrete square. The machine vibrated to a halt, the long blades swishing. The young orderly and the pilot pushed the

179

Hooligan-laden wheelchair out of the doorway, and winched it, revolving slowly, the five feet to the ground.

"Cummon," growled Hooligan. "Cut me loose of the damn bird."

The orderly unhooked the cable and began wheeling the chair in the direction of Hooligan's pointing finger.

Jumbo hissed over his shoulder: "If any shooting starts, make sure you get behind something solid. Just stay out of my way."

The orderly eyed Hooligan's broad back, and decided exactly what he'd do if any bullets started flying.

"Hurry," snapped Hooligan, pointing to a group of men standing near the bridge. Adam, holding a sub-machine-gun, ran to meet him. The orderly watched him arrive, saw the gun, let go of the handles of the chair and raised his arms above his head.

"Push," hissed Hooligan. "Push, you crazy nut. He's one of mine."

Adam panted over.

"You got everything how I want?" Hooligan demanded.

"Yup. And we can see some figures. Seem to be a lot of them. There's some inside the building, some outside with the truck, and a few in the bushes. I think they're shifting the bones."

"Right," said Jumbo. "Give me your special."

Adam pulled his police revolver from the holster on his belt. He passed it over to his chief. Hooligan flicked it open and spun the cylinder. "Don't lose it," said Adam. "It cost me money."

Hooligan ignored the jibe. "Tell everyone to get their lights ready. When I raise my arms, I want everything turned on. No shooting unless they open fire." He paused. "And tell the uniformed men not to perforate one of my boys this time."

He motioned to the orderly to start pushing again. "And make it real quiet," he told him. Nervously, the orderly padded forward. The wheelchair made a soft, crunching noise. Suddenly, Hooligan signalled him to stop. They could hear voices arguing by the derelict building ahead.

"But, madam, of course it's MY dinosaur ..."

"Absolutely nae proof, laddie ... yours isn't the ONLY dinosaur in the world, you know ... " Hooligan shuddered as he recognised the voice of the Scots nanny.

"What about our ten grand, then?"

Hooligan's eyes searched the gloom. He could make out darker than dark shadows amongst the trees. He looked out towards the river, the patrol boats were lined up in midstream, their bows pointing towards him. He glanced up at the bridge. It was lined with figures.

Hooligan whispered behind him. "Hold me up. I want to stand." He raised himself gingerly and balanced his weight on his good leg.

Jumbo Hooligan took a deep breath. Dressing gown flowing like biblical robes, he raised his arms in a God-like gesture. Miraculously it became daylight.

"Hold it, you there ..." he bawled. "This is the police. Freeeeeze."

*   *   *

Jumbo Hooligan wheeled himself across the office, spun the chair and wheeled it back again. His team lined the side walls, pistols drawn and held, resting on folded arms, penning Hooligan's captives.

"HA?" roared Jumbo. "A fine collection. All fresh from the hoosegow. Let me have a look at you. White collar workers ... nurses ... hobos ... and spies."

Una sneezed, loudly. Hooligan glared at her. "You, lady I know you've got to do it. But do it quietly." He swung his chair again and stopped in front of the museum official. "HA," he shouted, again. The man quivered.

"Er ... Mister Hooligan, you remember me. I'm from the museum ..."

"Mmmmm," said Jumbo. "So what were YOU doing down on the island? Excavating?"

"I ... er ... I had a tip-off." He pointed to Billie Big Canoe. "This man, Mr. Canute. He came and told me he'd found our dinosaur. We just went along to collect it."

"And, of course, you notified the police first. Hell, man, the 20th Precinct have been screwing this town inside out for the past week, trying to get those goddammed bones for you."

"I ... er ... forgot. The excitement," mumbled the embarrassed official.

"But you notified the Chinese."

"Of course ... er ... no. I'm afraid I don't know them. Just these three gentlemen, my colleagues. We went together."

"Okay," growled Jumbo. "Ivor, take those four outside. Get statements from them." He looked back at the museum official. "I'll want to see you again, later."

Ivor and the four men shuffled out of the room. Hooligan spun his wheelchair again and stopped it in front of Billie Big Canoe.

"Who are you ... ?"

"Billie Big Canoe, Chief," said Billie. "And this is my buddy, Herman." Herman nodded, wildly. "We was just along there with the museum man. We found the bones. We went and brought him back with us. Say, this won't affect the reward, will it? I mean, ten thou ..."

Hooligan held up his hand. "Huw, get these two outside. Statements again. And you'd better hold them until we check 'em out."

"Boss ... we ain't done nothin'. We was only helping," said Billie Big Canoe.

"How about trespass?" asked Jumbo Hooligan. He twisted himself in the wheelchair until he could view the five Chinese.

"Okay, Lui Ho. Spill it."

"Tourists," said Lui Ho, in pained English. "We are tourists over here on cultural mission. We visiting hospital on Welfare Island. Only to enquire as to entertainment

182

offered to inmates."

"Nuts," grunted Jumbo Hooligan.

"And, generally furthermore," continued Lui Ho, wearing his most innocent expression, "we claim special consideration, because we are exceedingly patriotic NATIONALIST Chinese—from Formosa. God bless Chiang Kai-Shek. Long may he reign over us. Hurrah for Imperialist dragon and for Nationalist Chinamen. And also, four cheers for America, for great kindnesses shown to our beloved Nationalist China."

"Crap," snarled Hooligan, remembering the hours spent debugging his office after the last visit paid by Lui Ho's team.

Jumbo Hooligan pushed himself up in his chair, so he could stare into Lui Ho's eyes behind the frosted lenses. "All right. ALL RIGHT. I know ALL about you, Lui Ho, and ALL about your stinking team of Reds. I know how you got here, and where you came from. And I know how you got your Nationalist visas. I've been waiting quite a while to put the finger on you." He paused. "So okay, you want to be REAL Nationalist Chinese! Well, that's how we'll treat you."

Lui Ho smiled with relief.

"And we'll send you *back* to *Nationalist* China."

Lui Ho's face bleached.

"We have some very, VERY good friends there. They're ALWAYS very happy to receive ex-patriots. You know, Lui Ho, I never have trouble with the Turks or the French. Why don't you Reds behave like the other spies?" Hooligan sighed. "I almost wish we were at war. Then I could have you shot here and now." He signalled Boots and Ulysses. "Get this load of crap out of my office. Get them down to Kennedy Airport. Don't let them collect or take anything with them. Get them on the first flight to Taipeh. AND have them escorted ALL the way. If they argue, chain 'em in the freight hold."

Lui Ho visualised a bare concrete cell, its walls painted

183

in yellow and black zig-zag stripes. And he thought of the early morning walk across the Nationalist Chinese courtyard—to a bullet-scarred wall.

Lui Ho played his last card. "One moment, Mister Jumbles Hooligan," he said. "I wish to make a bartering. To ask for political asylum. In exchange, I give complete information on Communist Chinese spy network Tse Eih Aei."

Hooligan looked at him with contempt. He thought of the Western agents killed by the Chinese organisation. "If it was Sam Ling asking, I could say yes. In fact, ANY of the others. Because THEY might be of some use to us. But you, Lui Ho—you're just a brainwashed, political thug. A Maoist zombie. YOU THINK NOTHING. Boots, get them on their way, NOW."

He waited until the door closed behind the spies, then he turned to the five nannies. "Ladies," he said, quietly. "I think the time has arrived for intimate conversation. If you play dumb," warned Hooligan, "I'll have you taken down and charged with conspiring with a Communist state. Then I'll have you locked away in little cells in The Tombs while I take a long vacation. Sometime, someone may just get round to wondering what happened to you all. Do I make myself clear?"

They nodded.

"Okay, we'll begin at the beginning. And, as far as I can see, the story begins on the steps of the museum. Right?"

The nannies stayed silent.

"So why did you steal the dinosaur?"

"For the emancipation of women ..." began Emily.

"Espionage ..." cut in Jumbo Hooligan. "The time is long gone for bedtime stories, nanny. I know WHY the dinosaur was stolen. Your British Secret Service has told us all about the man who died on the steps, and what he was doing in the museum. For God's sake, ladies, WE'RE ON THE SAME SIDE. Don't you see that?"

Melissa grimaced. "But we were told not to trust anyone."

Jumbo looked at them benignly. "You've got to trust me. So, suppose you tell me EXACTLY what happened? Every last detail."

"Er ..." Hettie spoke, cautiously. "Would you mind very much if we whispered together? We ken it's not really polite."

"You've got one minute," said Jumbo.

The nannies whispered.

Hettie looked at Hooligan again. "We've agreed," she told him. "We'll tell you all about it. But it was really all my fault."

"Lady," said Jumbo, calmly. "You didn't need to tell ME that."

Hettie spoke for half an hour. She began, and ended, with the same sentence. "We did it for our dear Queen and Country."

"Just one point I want to check," said Hooligan, when she'd finished. "Tell me again, exactly, what he said when he was dying."

"World security, and avoid total destruction ... museum ... the message ... microdot. And then he said, 'room thirteen ... the largest exhibit'."

"Hold it," said Hooligan. He pressed the button on his desk and called into the intercom. "Sheba, bring me in a guide book for the museum."

A few seconds passed, then the door opened and Sheba walked smoothly into the office. She handed her boss the book, and left.

Jumbo rested it on his knee and flipped the pages. "Ha ..." he exclaimed. "Women!" He looked at Hettie. "Did you buy a guide book?"

Hettie shook her head.

"Holy cow," said Jumbo Hooligan. "The museum authorities have a guide book printed, and five dames who want to knock off an exhibit don't even buy one. Don't misunderstand me, ladies. I got a lot of time for your patriotism. I like your guts. And boy, I sure envy you your

185

determination and energy. But, phew, you make lousy agents. Here ..." He held the book out to Hettie. "Take a close look at this." He pointed.

Hettie studied the floor plan. "Oh, heavens," she groaned. The four other nannies stared at her. "There are three room thirteens. One on every floor of the museum."

Hooligan smiled. "So, the largest exhibit in room thirteen could be any one of three things."

"Oh, dear," said Hettie. "So the message mightn't be in the dinosaur?"

"Almost certainly isn't," growled Jumbo Hooligan. "I've got some of the boys, in the basement right now, giving the bones the going-over. But, from what we know, the agent didn't have time to get up to the Early Dinosaur Hall to make his plant. My money's in one of the other two room thirteens."

"All that wasted energy," moaned Melissa.

"No ..." said Hooligan, brightly. "Not wasted. You didn't do THAT much of a bad job. In fact I'm pleased. You gave me the opportunity I needed to clear out these Red Chinese spies, and you kept them occupied chasing the wrong thing. Even if they'd got the dinosaur, they wouldn't have got the message. You didn't do a bad job at all."

"Thanks," said Hettie, quietly. Una was stifling another sneeze.

"Aw, cummon," said Jumbo. "Look, ladies, to show you how pleased I am, I'll let you come along to the museum with us and see if we can find that message. Then I'll take you all out to dinner. Right?" He banged a hand on each wheel of his chair. "I could sure use a professional buggy-pusher. Will you come?"

The nannies nodded.

"After we've put the bairns abed," said Hettie.

"Good God." Emily grabbed Hettie by the arm. "The children ... they're in the truck. We forgot them."

"No," said Jumbo. "Don't panic. They're down in the canteen. Sheba's laid on some food for them."

Hettie's eyes flared. "Food ..." she roared. "Canteen food? Police canteen food? Good gracious, NO! The poor wee darlings—they'll be poisoned." She drew herself up in front of Hooligan. "How dare you, laddie? How DARE you take it on yourself to interfere with our bairns? Wait until the British Embassy hears about this. I'll have you sacked. How dare you take liberties with British citizens, like this?"

Jumbo Hooligan held his head in his hands. "Screwballs," he sighed.

11

The invitation read: "His Excellency, the British Ambassador, requests the pleasure of the company of Mr. and Mrs. W. Badenberg, at a reception at the Carlyle Hotel, East 76th Street, on Friday, 17th of October, at 7.45 p.m. Guests are requested to bring their children, and children's nurses. Special facilities have been arranged."

"Oh, gee, Walt," gasped Mrs. Badenberg. "A reception at the Carlyle. Our first diplomatic invitation." She smiled at her husband. "I guess that means we're 'in'."

He raised his eyebrows.

"And it says here," she added, excitedly, "that decorations should be worn. Gee, you'll be able to wear that medal you won at the golf tournament last week."

Walter Badenberg groaned. "They mean WAR medals, honey. They want me to wear my war medals."

"Those dull old things. Wear the golf one as well. It's kind of pretty. And not EVERYBODY has one of those."

*　　*　　*

Randy Andy lay on his bed, looking up at the mirror on the ceiling, watching the sun-tanned young man staring down at him. He was in love with the redhead lying next to the man in the mirror. He fanned the air with his invitation.

"Of course, I shall go. We shall both go. After all, YOU'RE my nanny, and I'm YOUR employer. AND, the card IS addressed to me."

"It'll be very embarrassing," said Melissa. "I'll have to be in uniform, and you'll be in tails. And I shan't know if you should stay in an ante-room with the other children, or go in with the guests."

"I shall be a guest," said Randy.

"Pig."

Randy looked sideways at the tall mirrors on the walls on either side of the wide divan, with its smoky mirror bedhead. He twisted over and began undoing the buttons down the front of Melissa's blouse. He watched himself undressing her from a dozen different angles. It was erotic. A thousand diminishing beds on either side of him contained a man undressing a titian-haired girl. He peered at the reflecting bedhead. A broad-shouldered man was also undressing a girl. Randy could see right down her cleavage. He looked at the foot of the bed. In another mirror was the same couple. He glimpsed black stockings, and a pair of panties.

Randy watched the girl on the ceiling loosening the man's belt. Then her long, white fingers smoothed down the zip ... Randy turned his back to the audience above him.

"To hell with the lot of them," he mumbled.

It was dusk when Randy next looked at the line of beds beside him. Hundreds of naked and exhausted couples lay sweatily resting. A whole dormitory of them. He looked at the man in the headboard. The man winked at him and grinned. Randy grinned back.

*   *   *

The five nannies stood together in the banqueting room of the Carlyle Hotel in New York. Their uniforms gave a strange hospital look to the elegant surroundings, and the formally dressed guests.

"No taste," said Hettie, quietly, watching another couple walking in through the door. "She shouldn't wear tweed to an affair like this."

"Hush, Hettie," whispered Emily, sipping a cocktail that a waiter had offered her. She held the glass delicately with her left hand, and neatly adjusted a small bib around the throat of baby Lindon with her right. "I hope they hurry with the small sandwiches," she said. "I refuse to feed my children on canapes. And nuts and olives are bad for them."

"Certainly bad for them," agreed Una. She felt herself beginning a sneeze, pulled her handkerchief from her handbag, and had a quick sniff at the garlic clove that Vittorio Porcello had given her as a good-luck charm. She wished he was with her.

There was a sudden, sharp rapping. "Ladies and gentlemen," called a voice. "Pray silence for His Excellency, the British Ambassador."

The diplomat stood beside a door at the farthest end of the huge room. His voice was rich and deep. With some surprise, the nannies noticed that Jumbo Hooligan was standing beside him.

"Ladies and gentlemen," began the Ambassador. "I hope that you'll all forgive my informality in welcoming you like this. I know that it is a little early for speeches, but there is a special reason for your being here tonight. And, because it is a special reason, I have to say these few words first." He turned and whispered to Hooligan. The big man smiled.

"We have some very important people here tonight," continued the Ambassador.

"I told you," preened Mrs. Badenberg to her husband.

"They are standing over there." The Ambassador pointed across the room to the nannies. Susanne looked behind her. There was nothing but the wall. "The very important people are those five nurses."

There was a surprised murmur from the guests.

"Not only important to you, as the custodians of your children, but important to their country, Great Britain. I am sure that none of you are aware that, recently, they have all, by great enterprise, courage and determination, served the Western world in the highest and most noble manner. Security prevents me from giving you full details. All I may say, is that the United States government appreciated their assistance, and relayed its thanks, officially, back to Whitehall. Her Majesty, Queen Elizabeth the Second, has seen fit to make a special award." He turned to an aide, who held out a small bundle of white packets.

"Nanny Hettie MacPhish," called the aide. Hettie blushed, and walked towards the Ambassador. He shook her hand and smiled. He reached forward and she felt him pin something on the stiff front of her uniform. She curtsied and started to walk back.

"Just one minute, ma'am," grinned Jumbo Hooligan. He held out an envelope towards her. "Token of appreciation from the United States Government." Hettie took it and curtsied again. Hooligan's mouth grinned even wider. He wondered how each of the nannies would spend the five-thousand dollar Government cheques.

Hettie's face tingled. She knew it was red. She felt hot and flushed as she walked towards her friends. She heard the Ambassador's aide call Emily's name. Hettie risked a quick look down at the thing pinned to her uniform. She felt a lump harden in her throat. Gleaming, on the starched uniform, was the Silver Greyhound, the badge of the Queen's Couriers.

* * *

It had been a long hard winter. Snow had fallen in New York until March. The ponds in the park were still frozen and New Yorkers, collars up, hat brims down, sludged their way from subway to offices and home. Spring was late, but it arrived today. Herman, the hobo, welcomed it back.

"Hi, bum," he called to a lone grey squirrel which

haunched in front of his seat, waiting for him to toss some of his biscuit crumbs. "Here comes the sun."

The squirrel grabbed an untrusting mouthful and scampered to the shelter of a tree. The buds were hatching new-green, undusted by the city traffic.

Herman reached into his coat. "Hey, Euclid, how you doin' in there?" He pulled out his varicoloured snake. Euclid coiled his tail round Herman's forearm and wriggled back into the jacket and the attraction of the hobo's warm chest. "Come on out and see the park," commanded Herman, dragging the snake back into the open. "Show your shiny collar."

Just behind the snake's head, on the slimmest part that was nearly a neck, a thin gold band encircled him.

"Ain't you pretty," said Herman, stroking the snake's sleek sides. "And ain't you got just the prettiest clothes? Real gold clothes." He looked down. His own Fifth Avenue tuxedo was crumpled by nights of sleeping rough. The *New York Times*, which had served, complete, as a blanket during the night, lay on the pathway in front of him. He stared. A familiar face stared back. It was Billie Big Canoe, in the centre of a flock of pretty girls in the foyer of the Plaza Hotel. Herman nudged the newspaper with his foot for a moment, then pulled it to reading distance. The caption to the photograph read: "Wall Street's wonder tycoon, William Longship, celebrating another coup today in negotiating the takeover of Alsop's New West Supertraderies."

Herman sighed. He thought back. Days of riotous high life with the jet-set. A trip to Europe. Cocktails, dinner and breakfasts with his former socialite idol, Hazel Willingboddy—from whom he'd caught gonorrhoea in St. Moritz. That was before his dinosaur money ran out.

"Goddam me, Billie." Herman smiled sadly at the newspaper picture. "You always said I was a foolish virgin ... but I wonder if you'd stake me fifty bucks?"

Memorandum

FROM: The pen of your enlightened Chairman
      Mao Tse-tung.
TO: The Department of Geophysical
      Research, Peking Academy of Sciences.

Comrades:

Regretfully, and due to its unfortunate
exposure, I have had to cancel my brilliant
stratagem to destroy the Capitalist West
by means of our Great Leap Downward.

However, as I said in my speech of
February 27th, 1957, which you no doubt
recall, it is "sheer fantasy to imagine that
the cause of Socialism is all plain sailing
and easy success, without difficulties and
setbacks, or the exertion of tremendous
efforts".

I now propose to approach the problem from
another direction. This plan will be
known as the Great Leap Inwards. The duty of
your Department is to supply me with the
precise date, hour, minute and second when
I should signal our beloved population of
750,000,000 to jump simultaneously into the
Pacific Ocean, thereby causing maximum
water-displacement which will . . .